© Shami Gee

---

*About the Author*

---

JONNY GLYNN is a British writer and actor who has written for the stage and the screen and has performed in dozens of plays, including the Royal Shakespeare Company's complete works of Shakespeare program. He lives in London with his wife and daughter.

# THE SEVEN DAYS OF PETER CRUMB
## JONNY GLYNN

HARPER PERENNIAL

NEW YORK • LONDON • TORONTO • SYDNE`

HARPER ● PERENNIAL

'Mister Cellophane,' words by Fred Ebb and music by John Kander, copyright © 1975 Unichappell & Co. Inc. and Kander & Ebb Inc. All rights administered by Warner/Chappell Music Ltd., London W6 8BS. Reproduced by permission.

Epigraph from *The Gulag Archipelago* by Alexander Solzhenitsyn, published by the Harvill Press. Reprinted by permission of the Random House Group.

First published in Great Britain in 2007 by Portobello Books Ltd.

FIRST U.S. EDITION

Library of Congress Cataloging-in-Publication Data is available upon request.

ISBN: 978-0-06-135148-8

08 09 10 11 12  ID/RRD  10 9 8 7 6 5 4 3 2 1

If only there were evil people somewhere insidiously committing evil deeds, and it were necessary only to separate them from the rest of humanity and destroy them. But the line dividing good and evil cuts through the heart of every human being. And who is willing to destroy a piece of his own heart?

**Alexander Solzhenitsyn**

I am not a good man.
I am not a bad man.
In seven days I will be dead.
My name is Peter Crumb.



This is what remains…

# MONDAY

Write it down, he said – every dirty word, he said – the truth of it – the awful evil truth of it.

I woke in a shocking condition. My body livid with dehydration. My mind exquisitely deranged. That numb ache and the awful prospect, another day...

Straight away I could feel him, on me, and in me, that damp and familiar presence, disjoining through me, wringing me out, twisting the tired stiffened ends of me apart, distending his limbs long through mine, acknowledging cognizance, and yawning.

'Good morning,' he drooled. A tired wet slur of lazy vowels and sneering bonhomie... His breath was of the kidney, it is always of the kidney.

I ignored him, kicked at my slippers and shuffled off into

the kitchen. He followed me, whistling. I recognized the tune immediately. It was a tune my father used to whistle. A cheery, seven-dwarfs-off-to-work sort of whistle. Quite terrifying. I filled the kettle and smelt the milk.

'Breakfast,' he said, pulling up a chair and joining uninvited, 'will be neither English nor Continental. Just two slices of stale brown bread – lightly toasted, smeared with rancid unsalted yellow fat and topped with cheap gollywog preserve.'

It was as if he was trying to impress me. I paid him no mind, lit a cigarette and sat perfectly still, my eyes fixed staring at the shadow between the edge of the table and the wall. I held my gaze unblinking until the kettle reached its climax. It almost had him fooled, for a moment I felt normal and everyday, but it was no use, the cigarette had worked its magic, my guts were churning, and he knew it –

'I feel the pinch,' he cried, 'and am ready to shit.'

I bolted for the toilet, my bowels voiding. Grade 7 on the Bristol, I'm afraid to say – 'sloppy, no solid pieces', just a cloudy smattering of unctuous yellow viscidity, spat out of my arse all over the bowl, quite disgusting. The vile fetid stink of faecal waste was all about me, inside and out – I was gagging. 'Christ,' he said, 'I can taste it.' And he wasn't joking. I then found I had no toilet tissue. 'Bloody marvellous,' he said. I didn't panic, I kept a straight face and played the Hindu. I squatted in the bathtub, ran my arse under the tap and used my left hand. All in all it was quite refreshing.

Afterwards, as I was drying off, I caught sight of him in the mirror, watching me… Shifty and venal, guilty and afraid… I looked away, ashamed.

My skin is green. I smell of mould. The scab on my ankle is weeping… What would Mother say? Clean your teeth.

'My toothpaste,' he said, picking it up and squeezing out a pea-sized blob, 'is herbal. Camomile, sage, eucalyptus and myrrh. It combines the oral-care science of Colgate with nature's best herbs and claims to protect the whole family.'

From what? I thought.

'The contempt these people hold you in,' he said. 'Doesn't it rile? Implicit in their claim to protect the whole family is the notion that your family is in danger.' And then he looked at me, brought his face close to mine and whispered – warning me, he whispered, 'Do not swallow.'

I sluiced with warm water. He doesn't like cold, it hurts his teeth.

In my jacket, as I was getting dressed, I found an old photograph of Emma. A twisted scrap of recollection, forgotten in a pocket. A girl on a beach with a bucket and spade, four years old, sticky beneath the sunshine, blushing ice-cream smiles. A mummy and daddy. Happy and whole. And unembarrassed. To think that was once my life… She'd be fourteen on the 28th of April.

My eyes were misting, my throat lumping, emotions mobilizing, and he was on me, snatching the photograph from my fingers. 'I don't forget,' he said. 'I'm very good at memory.' And then he tore the picture into tiny pieces and scattered them all over the carpet and barked, 'Remember that? Remember that?'… I do remember that. It left me shaking… The long arm was east, the short arm west… He went and stood in the corridor and made that munching noise, and then watched the cleaning lady through the spyhole in the front door. She comes once a month and pushes a hoover around the communal parts and gives it all a bit of a tidy. I don't know her name – I've never actually spoken to her – but I think she may be foreign. She has the gormless dewy-eyed look of an Eastern European about her, but he thinks she may be a Cockney – I'm not so sure. He said he could smell her and that she smelt cheap. He said she had a sour little mouth, pinched tight shut like a cat's arse. And then he put his hand in my pocket and tweaked the end of my penis. He said there was something about her guttersnipe demeanour that he found profoundly arousing. He said he imagined her to be an accomplished sexualist, exhaustively perverse in the bedroom, a cider-drinking reader's wife that knows no shame – a real dirty banger, he said – yes, he said, fiddling his fingers in my pocket, pinching the end of me. Sex among the common classes is so of itself, so *sui generis* – their uncles break them in at an early age and then they're at it every day after. She's probably seen more cock than the public lavatories in King's Cross station... And then he said I should rape her... He said she'd love it, that that kind of thing would be sport to a girl like her... He said that Nietzsche – or it might have been Oscar Wilde, or James Bond – once said, *'A woman hath no greater love, than that she hath for the first man that raped her.'*

I stared at the wall and pretended not to notice as he wanked me.

It was weird... Just at the moment of coming, the telephone started to ring. It took me quite by surprise and ruined the moment for him. It rang fifteen times and then fell silent. He didn't answer it, he just stood there staring at it, his trousers around his ankles, his cock twitching, oozing thick globs of the ivory white, sticky and clean between his thumb and fore-finger, a hoover groaning in the corridor. I remember thinking that if it wasn't all so terrifying it might almost have been amusing – 'And this, Your Majesty, is *Homo sapiens*...' He didn't laugh, he looked aggrieved, shoved his hand in my mouth and ordered me to lick the spunk from his fingers. I didn't want to anger him, I instinctively understand that he is not a man that one should anger, and so I dutifully obeyed him and greedily gobbled and licked his gummy fingers clean. They tasted of... marmalade? Then he ordered me to dial 1471. Withheld number. 'Typical,' he said. I wondered who it was, but he said it didn't matter, and that all that was behind me now, and that soon 'I'll be cut off.'

He looked at me menacingly. He seemed resentful, and hurt ... I said nothing, and my silence seemed to defeat him. He went and sat in the kitchen by himself and made one of his drawings. I watched him for exactly seven minutes, wrestling with himself, muttering and scribbling. I don't know why, but I suddenly felt profoundly sorry for him. He lives without hope, I thought, and sees nothing but infinite sadness in all that sur-rounds him... Poor bugger. In seven days he will be dead, and there is nothing I can do for him... I realize he has a deep-seated loathing of human beings, and I understand that obvi-ously that is going to be a problem if you live on the planet earth, but I cannot help him. I fear men and hate women. In seven days I will be dead.

North by north-west. Lolloping in the front room, with a jazz cigarette. The curtains drawn, the light a dirty mustard yellow. Outside, Night's militant brother, Day, pushy, loud and everywhere. Inside, a one-lit-bulb electric gloom, and a warm soft after-wank calm, conspiring inward...

*Hashish, hashish, the morning yawned,*
*Her sweet blue smoke ascending.*
*Hashish, hashish, the morning yawned,*
*A dark neurotic curling.*

I wrote it down. It was a mistake – I shouldn't have. It made him angry, very angry. He wildly protested: 'I resent these pretentious artistic affectations! They're a perversion. They unteach and obscure. They mean nothing!'

And then he stormed out of the room and slammed the door. I could hear him in the corridor, moving things, and muttering, in and out of every room, banging doors. It made me feel very anxious. Choices were gnawing at my innards, thoughts mustering, dark and fearful. Cold, distracted, paranoid judgements, abusing me. What to do? My heart was beating... What to do?

'Get out of the house!' he stormed. 'Get out of the house!' Harrying me and slamming doors. I didn't think to question, but it was a mistake. I shouldn't have listened. The last thing I should have done was leave the house.

South by north-north-west. Tucked into a corner of Don's Café on the Lower Clapton Road, two fried eggs in front of me.

'Don't eat them,' he said.

'Why not?' I said.

'They've been tampered with,' he said. 'Look at them – one yolk is yellow, the other yolk is orange. What am I supposed to make of that?'

He was right. Some pervert scientist had obviously had his hand down the front of their genetic underpants and given them a little tickle.

'Look at them!' he said. 'Paedofiddlized eggs on toast! First thing in the morning! How dare you! The yellow yolk bleeds thin, but the orange yolk doesn't.'

He looked at me with an outraged, disgusted indignation, drew his mouth up, sneering beneath his nostrils, and said, 'If it is that my eggs are to be served from a sex offender's register, I will in future take them scrambled.'

It was so embarrassing. A man at another table was watching me, I caught his eye, it was obvious what he was thinking, he looked away. I saw the hairs on the back of my hand, prickling.

'Right,' he said, tweaking the tips of my fingers. 'Let us begin.'

Lying, folded, face down in front of me, was that greasy wad of righteous indignation, the *Daily Mail*.

'We always take the *Mail* on a Monday,' he said. 'And so it will be today.'

I picked it up. A gouged breathless dread stopped in my throat. He smiled, that malignant sneer. The headline in the paper read:

# MURDER

'Amen,' he said. 'My course is set.'

Left Don's, and ambled on… To and fro, and up and down…
Looking, seeing, and thinking.

On Victoria Park Road he stopped and told me to go and look in
a dustbin. It was a revolting, stinking, overflowing eruption of
oily filth and thrown-out crap, but I got stuck in, regardless of
the bolt-eyed morons watching me as they lumbered past – disgusted, pitying and contemptuous.

'Seek and ye shall find,' he kept repeating. 'Seek and ye
shall find.'

And oh dear God what a thing it was he found. About
halfway down, covered in barbecue ketchup, and the sucked remains of chewed Dixie fried chicken wings, he found a large
steel hammer with a rubber grip and broken claw. He pulled it
out, stuffed it into my pocket, winked at me and whispered,
'The means.'

I followed him into the park.

It was a beautiful day. The sun was shining and the daffodils
were all in bloom, trumpeting their happiness. Mothers with
children out playing. The world seemed perfectly at ease with
itself. I should have been feeling the same, but didn't. Yellow
and blue have returned to the garden. But returned too soon.

'I have been awake for four hours and forty-five minutes,'
he said, 'but it feels longer.' I said I agree. He said he suffered
from permanent feelings of tiredness. I said that's as maybe,
which seemed to confuse him and shut him up… I sat on a
bench and stared… There was silence and then he said – he
said, 'In seven days I will be dead, but for seven days I will be
free. Free to realize my potential as a human being, as a man, in

whatever wonderful or dreadful a way that that might be…'
And then he paused, sweating, and said, 'Traditionally hammers are used to bang nails… I mean, you know… murder who?'

A skinny little Bangladeshi, that's who… I looked up, and she sat down, no more than seventeen. Why did I look up? Straight away his eyes were on her – watching her, sideways, glancing, unobserved, taking note. 'Skinny,' he said, 'isn't she? Very skinny. A brittle, matchstick, snap-in-two sort of skinny – isn't she?' he said. 'A not nice Auschwitz thin,' he said. 'Clearly disordered. Remarkable these humans… These stupid humans…'

She was dressed in black jeans, Puma trainers and a purple striped sports shirt of no particular allegiance. Her hair was dark and lank and rolled to her shoulders forming a natural hood that shrouded her face and darkened her pointed rat-like features, pocked and marked with the battle scars of adolescent pus wars. She was nibbling a sandwich, it looked fishy, possibly tuna, and drinking a can of Sprite lite. She kept looking at her mobile, expecting it to ring, but it didn't. She smoked Lambert & Butler. The cigarette supersized in her skeleton grip. She swallowed the smoke instead of inhaling. 'A learner,' he said. 'Yes, I will follow her.'

He likes following people. Keeping a casual distance. Not being noticed. Letting yourself be led. 'Let's see where she leads me,' he said. 'Come on.'

I knew what he was going to do, and I knew what he was going to do it with. I remember thinking – is she the one he's going to do it to?… I wasn't so sure.

15

I followed him, following her, for about half a mile to a newsagent's on Sudder Street, where it appeared she worked. He loitered outside, watching her through the window, standing bored behind the counter. Seventeen years of brittle aggression, reading *Heat* and sulking.

'Leave this to me,' he said, pushing me aside and entering the shop. I dithered in the doorway for a moment and then joined him at the counter.

'Good morning, my dear,' he began, with the oiled charm of a game-show host. What's he doing, I thought, putting on these ridiculous airs? He calls it his menials demeanour, the swine – who does he think he is? The girl looked at him oddly.

'A packet of Drum, please, my love,' he continued unabated. I can't believe he called her 'my love'. She turned, found the tobacco, tossed it disdainfully onto the counter and fingered the till.

'Two nineteen,' she spat. No please, no thank you, she didn't even look at him. I liked her style. He rummaged in my pocket, found the appropriate coins and handed them to her. She dropped the coins into the till and returned to the glossy gurning Jade, Brad and Jen. At this juncture in the commercial exchange it would have been normal to thank her and leave, but he didn't, he just stood there, staring at her, hand on hammer in pocket, wondering: Are you the one?

And then something happened – I think I may have briefly dissociated. The next thing I remember she was looking at me, and speaking. Her tone was indignant and demanding – 'D'you want something? D'you want something?' She kept repeating it – it was quite odd. And then I remember I felt my mouth slowly peel into a twisted grimace, my lips blistering dry against teeth too stained to care, and I heard him say: 'I think you're a red herring.'

Confusion twitched between her eyebrows. She was scared. He tossed her a cheeky wink, withdrew my toothy grin and left. We sighed a sigh… He said she's not the one…

I ambled on, distracted, bored, confused, at sixes and sevens, looking for a sign and wondering where. I hopped onto the 38 bus and settled into my favourite seat, right at the back on the top deck. I watched the carnival parade of Hackney grim clamber on and shuffle off. The poor ugly batches of humanity that grubble up on public transport – immigrants, aliens and Oyster-card holders. All God's own – the awful rabble. I closed my eyes, folded myself away and jostled off into a gentle doze.

When I woke two monkey schoolgirls were sat in front of me, kissing their teeth and cursing a girl called Jamilla. Their conversation went something as follows:

'I's gonna fuck dat bitch up man.'

'D'you get me?'

'Who da fuck does she fink she is man?'

'D'you know what I mean?'

'Fucking bitch cuss me.'

'I's gonna fuck 'er up bad boy.'

'You know what I'm sayin'?'

'For real you kna.'

'I ain't muckin' abart.'

'Fucking bitch innit?'

'Me say to her – Allow it lady.'

'Fuckin' byatch.'

'You know what I mean?'

'My cousin know 'er and she ain't never even been to Camberwell.'

'Get on the number two lady.'

'D'you get me?'

'Fuckin' bitch.'

'Kiss your teef at me –'

'Fuckin' bitch. '

I could feel my anger thickening, lumping into indignation. Stewing and fuming through their purple-gummed, foul-mouthed excess until I could take it no more. How dare they?

'Excuse me,' I blurted, my fingers prodding her shoulder, 'but could you please stop swearing.' A perfectly reasonable and politely put request I thought. But no –

'Don't you fuckin' touch me!' the first one spat. 'Fuckin' pokin' my shoulder.'

'Well, would you please stop swearing,' I persisted.

'Who da fuck's it gotta do wiv you?' the other one chipped in.

'Pokin' my shoulder.'

'Tell me what I can do.'

'Fuckin' pokin' my shoulder.'

'Oo da fuck is you to fuckin' tell me? – I ain't told by you.'

'Fuckin' pokin' my shoulder.'

'You should have some respect and consideration for the other passengers,' I endeavoured.

'What respec you giving me? Fuckin' pokin' my shoulder – oo da fuck are you?'

'Fuckin' respec – you's a fuckin' homeless boy.'

People were turning and watching. Looking at me. I could feel myself blushing. The girls were triumphant. Their faces were screwed into a hideous gnarl, their teeth spitting kisses. They knew they'd won. They knew there was nothing I could do to stop them. And they knew nobody would come to my rescue. They had me cornered and were going in for the kill.

'Oo da fuck are you?!'

'Pokin' my shoulder.'

'Don't fuckin' tell me what I can do.'

'I fuckin' say what I fuckin' like – innit.'

'Hello – is a fuckin' democracy.'

'Pokin' my shoulder? Tell me I 'ave respec.'

'I don't get fuckin' told by fuckin' no-one – not by my teacher – not by my mum not by fuckin' no-one. I say what I like cos that's the way I am innit – I is oo I is. You don't know nuffin abart me. And you fink you can call on me. You's a fool boy. Show me I.'

'Pokin' my shoulder!'

'Fuckin' tramp man.'

'Fuckin' stinkin of piss boy.'

'Tell me what I do.'

'Pokin' my shoulder.'

'Piss boy.'

And so they went on. I was humiliated. And everyone was watching. The whole bus saw it – heard every word of it, but said nothing. And did nothing. My face was burning – blushing raw embarrassed shame. I had been utterly debased. It was awful. I stood up, timid and afraid. Yes, I was afraid – afraid, can you believe? – of two schoolgirls. Afraid, defeated and shat on.

I shuffled forward to descend the stairs and get off the bus, but the girls weren't through with me yet, they turned and fired one last salvo – 'Yeah you betta get off paedo, before I tell the Popo.' And then they started laughing. Laughing with the unrestrained, unembarrassed joy that only children know. I put my eyes to the floor. It was awful. Everyone was watching. All eyes were on me. I was filled with shame. I wanted to lash out and hurt them. Hurt them all. Hurt every gutless one of them. Sat there, with their sneering lips and half-cocked eyebrows. Have at my hammer and hack at them all. The bus was hurtling down Rosebery Avenue. 'Cowards!' I started to shout, but lost courage halfway through and quickly converted my deranged scream into a coughing sound. But the cough came out confused and sounded like the noise you make when you're trying to stop yourself from crying. It was pathetic, awful, and utterly humiliating… A woman, a *woman*, looked at me with pity and disdain… I shuffled off, and ambled on… Poor Crumb.

He said that it was pointless trying to communicate with the social underbelly. They're savages, he said – wild untamed savages. There's no use trying to reason with them, they don't know any better. You should pity them, he said. Their fathers were probably absent, and they only ever eat fried chicken, imagine that for a lifetime. They're Special Needs, he said – you want to give them a chance – a weekend in the country is all they need, mud all over their trainers and they'll soon come to their senses. You were probably the same at their age – a cheeky little monkey answering back, playing the fool, getting up to mischief…

But I wasn't. I was a good boy. I was quiet and did what I was told. I had a mother and a father. Present every day. We ate meals together around a table. They taught me the difference between right and wrong, good manners from bad. They set the correct pattern of behaviour and liaised with my teachers to ensure that my homework was always of the highest standard and in on time. They taught me to respect my elders, not tell them to fuck off... You're privileged, he said, and blessed to have been born into the middle classes. You should know better, he said. You've no excuses... I ambled on at pace, shooing myself away, grinding my teeth. I was hot and completely inappropriately dressed, as usual. I felt worried and anxious and paranoid. My skin was tight. That goading feeling was there again, twisted in my innards, working me into a state. I was sweating and people were looking.

'They can smell you, Crumb – they can smell you.' He kept repeating it. 'They can smell you, Crumb.' Goading me, kindling that rage within, that hatred – that petty bitter hatred that's vicious and mean, bristling and frenzied... I was stalking like a madman out of all control, this way and that – up Regent Street, and Piccadilly, through Green Park and St James's, into Parliament Square, and then up Whitehall, past Montgomery, Allenbrook and Slim – left right, left right... Tired out and trodden off, my legs like sautéed leeks – the pavement arguing and answering back every step of the way, and people everywhere, under my feet. Dawdling great apes. I stopped in Trafalgar Square, took in the sights and rolled another jazz. What a horrifying place Trafalgar Square is – full of freakshow gawping youth and holiday-of-a-lifetime losers, pigeons shitting everywhere... Kiss me Hardy and think of England...

I scuttled off and took refuge in the National Gallery…
'Where the Peach and I first kissed, and were in love.'

The Peach that he refers to was a girl called Valerie Cheatle.
We were in love. I know – doesn't that sound ridiculous? – in
love. How many times must I have uttered those words in sorry
excuse. It almost makes me want to vomit. It was a long time
ago now but the memory of it all still haunts. How does one
forget? We would idle away hours in galleries, wandering corridors, paddling palms and pinching fingers, kissing… When
was I last kissed? I remember it all meant so much to me, love.
And being in love…

All of this reflection, and all of this living – why do I indulge
it? Excuses and pardons from the past to the present.
Yesterday's apologies for tomorrow's mistakes. All of it very re-
grettable, I know that – oh yes, I've plenty to regret. I was only
a boy, you say – a mere youth, you say, engaged in the usual
youthful travails, you say – setting out on my journey, making
my way, deluding myself into thinking that there was something more to all of this – something more to all of me.
Well there isn't, and there won't be, and there wasn't. I was
the same from the start – and will be to the end – the Alpha
and the Omega – as was, is now, and ever shall be – lies and
lies and more lies – all lies – stuff and things and thoughts and
nonsense. The drivelling joke of it. The obfuscating farce of it!

But I digress… The Pre-Raphaelites were mooning – I felt
hot, my ankle was itching, people were looking, there were
noises I couldn't identify – my thoughts were jumbled, I
needed to get out, I was dying for a piss… Bladderwrack, I remember thinking, is a type of seaweed. My father showed me

how you can wear it like a wig and be a sea monster. I associate this memory with the image of nicotine-stained lower incisors and red receding gums, which for some reason reminds me that I once killed a frog. I killed it with a penknife. Whatever happened to that knife? Dad brought it back from Spain. It was a present – a masculine present – something to treasure and hold onto and not lose. Something to pass down through the generations and say, 'My father gave me that and now I'm giving it to you. Hold onto it, son – one day *you* may need to kill a frog.' It had a green and yellow handle and was shaped like a fish. The bucket was blue, I remember that. Yes. I drove it straight down through the frog's back and into the ground. The frog didn't make a sound. It was a horrid sight. I don't remember feeling anything. I went home and ate a Penguin. I didn't tell anyone. It was a sordid guilty secret. Many more of those now. Sordid furtive dirty unspeakable secrets. All the things we don't tell. That's who we are. I left the knife in the frog – that's right. I told Dad that Geoffrey Webb had stolen it. He told Geoff's parents and there was a scene. Geoff started crying and said I was lying. I came clean and said I'd lost it. Dad was disappointed and said I'd let him down. Mum stood in the doorway holding a plate of chilled chocolate digestives… We all felt ashamed… But again, I digress…

I was standing in the Wolfson Room admiring Nattier's Manon Balletti – she's so beautiful. In spite of the fact that she looks so like Valerie I cannot help returning to her. She has all the qualities I admire in a woman – stillness, quiet and a touch of pink. I lost myself looking at her and I think I may have dissociated. People were looking at me… I think I might have been thinking out loud, but I can't for certain recall. The long arm pointed north, the short arm south, I remember that. Rush hour had started. Everyone was busying and bustling home. I was sitting in Cranley Gardens drinking a can of lager, trying to compose myself. There had been an 'episode'… I let him get the better of me. Somewhere between the National Gallery and Cranley Gardens he urinated in my trousers. I don't know when or where exactly this happened, but I fear it may have been on the Tube. When I think of Oxford Circus, I think of the word 'purling'. How embarrassing. I bet everyone was looking at me and laughing – disgusted. They'll all be at home now, telling their nearest and dearest about a strange man they saw on the Tube – a revolting degenerate pervert, pissing his pants and rambling on about frogs and penknives and Manon Balletti and God only knows what else. Poor Peter Crumb, the unwitting star of a hundred anecdotes told at teatime to children as a warning of what will become of them if they don't do well at school… Poor Crumb – the fool… But again, I digress.

I was sitting in Cranley Gardens… the afternoon was at an end and the evening drawing in. It had been a weird day, and there was still the small matter of murder to contend with. My trousers were damp and heavy, like soggy cardboard, and my spirits the same. I was bored and felt lonely. I caught myself sighing, and that's always a bad sign. I wanted someone to talk to… He told me to shut up. He enjoys these petty assaults – it's how he engages. I sat in silence for some time, just watching and listening, smoking fags and smelling the air. And then I saw a man, an itinerant, shuffling from one litter bin to another and having a good old rummage. He was wearing a green cotton baseball cap, a worn stained duffel coat, blue Adidas tracksuit bottoms, red socks and open-toed sandals. He looked faintly ridiculous, but vaguely familiar... A kindred spirit? I thought. I gave him a nod as he wandered by and offered him a can of lager. It was a mistake. He was a revolting drunk, sodden in misery and almost certainly insane. A dirty old mumper of the lowest order. Slurping and burping, reeking of neglect, muttering thankyous and offering God's blessings – I don't know what I was thinking. The moment he sat down I was immediately reminded of what an uncomfortable arrangement talking to human beings is, so I said nothing – just fell silent, and thankfully so did he. We sat there tipping our cans and belching, legs crossed, ankles rotating, both of us quite separate. It's sad, we are all of us separate and there's no getting away from it. He finished his can and asked me if I had a fag. I lied and said no, even though I was smoking one. He got the message. He gave his can one last licking, stood up, paused, looked at me for a moment and then said – it amazed me – he said:

'Right then, must get on, that scab on my ankle's been weeping all morning.'

I couldn't believe it. I looked at him and he winked at me, nodded towards the hammer poking out of my pocket, smiled, opened his duffel coat and discreetly showed me a seven-inch screwdriver he had tucked into his belt.

'My aunt Sally gim in that.' Whatever that meant. He winked again, smiled again, brought the edge of his hand to the middle of his forehead, made a gurgling noise and went on his way. Poor old bugger, I thought. Crackers in the community, out wandering the streets, half his mind in pieces … The dirty old mumper.

Shuffle on, Crumb. Shuffle on and don't look back. Go to the pub. Buy a pint. Stand next to the radiator, get warm and dry your trousers… I ambled on to the Newman Arms.

A pint of black-and-tan, hot air, healthy smoke-filled back-slapping pubbery. A quiet corner, City Prices and my horror scope. Cheers.

## Aries

*As an Aries you are both patient and resourceful.*

Yes, I am.

*This means that when faced with a challenge you'll act first and assess the situation later …*

I see. Is that a good thing or a bad thing?

*However, it's worth taking into account the fact that certain individuals –*

Hello –

*Who were previously involved –*

Go on –

*If not very helpful –*

Yes –

*Will expect to be asked for their assistance again … ?*

*Certain individuals who were previously involved, if not very helpful, will expect to be asked for their assistance again …*

He put down his pint. His heart was beating, his skin tickled, he felt deliciously alive.

My trousers were dry. I returned to Sudder Street. The short arm pointed south-south-west, the long arm north-north-east. I knew what I was going to do… There was no denying it, or stopping it. I was going to murder the skinny Bangladeshi girl. I was going to murder her because the headline in the paper said so, he found a hammer, she entered on cue and Shelley von Strunckel agreed.

As I re-entered the newsagent's a crumpled sack of old age was standing at the counter, wheezing, reeking of potatoes and muttering something about having her card recharged. Skinny was serving. She glanced at me. I drooled a happy 'Hello.' She looked away, embarrassed, pretending not to remember, but she knew all right, she knew. The sack, its business done, slurped and shuffled out. I waited, patiently held in a dislocated calm. The shop was empty. The street outside on hold. Everything had stopped. Darkness gathered at the edges.

I smiled, taking my time, oiling my charm, that spiteful malevolent sneer unfolding. I inhaled deeply – in through my nose, and out through my mouth – seven, eight, nine, ten… Pause… 'We meet again.'

She held my stare. Her little rat-mouth, snapping back, 'D'you want something?'

'Ah ha,' he said. 'An offer of assistance.'

'What?'

'Can I help? Yes, you can – I'm looking for the answer to a riddle.'

She was freaked. 'What are you on about?'

'It started this morning at twenty past eight. The long arm east, the short arm west. A melodrama in three acts.'

'D'you want something or not?'

I was starting to enjoy myself – I could feel his limbs loosening, letting me in.

'Can I get you something or not?' Her fear was taking hold.

'I have a verb.'

'What?'

'Murder.'

The word seemed to jolt her, like a punch to the chest. She moved her hands to her hips – posturing, belligerent.

'Do you want to buy something or not? Cos if you're not going to buy something can you get out of the shop please.'

'Tell me, was your sandwich tuna?'

'What?' You could see the fear flickering through her. 'Can you get out of the shop please!' She stroppily demanded.

'You should feel lucky,' I heard myself saying. 'The other fella had a screwdriver. I've only got a hammer.'

And then she saw it, and the penny dropped. She knew. In that moment, she knew. I turned up the gas. 'Certain individuals who were previously involved, if not very helpful, will expect to be asked for their assistance again.'

She tried to scream, but the fear wouldn't let her.

'As an Aries I am both patient and resourceful.'

'You're a fuckin' nutter!'

'Yes, I am.'

'Mum!'

There it was – the line had been crossed – she was abandoning herself to desperate pleas. I remember thinking: these are her final words. I stepped behind the counter, trapping her, four feet between us. I could smell her.

'When faced with a challenge I'll act first and assess the situation later.'

'Mum!!'

'Don't be afraid.'

'Please!'

'Shit in your pants and that's how they'll find you!'

Wallop! I swung my arm with all my might and I buried that hammer right in her face, just above her left eye. I swung it with my heart and soul and smashed it straight through her skull and buried it in her brain – mashing it into a pulp. She went straight down and lay there, contorted and tangled. Twitching. Thick dark black blood pouring out of her… I watched her for about a minute, I think… Just watched her, silently dying. It seemed never to end. Get on with it, I thought, die. I lifted the hammer and clattered it down into her face a second time. I didn't need to. It was a mercy blow, to put her out of her misery. Her skull split in two. Her skin was ripped and… her features deformed and broken and mutilated… I just stood there looking at her and thought, right, that's that then… There you are … dead… You're dead now, and that's that.

At this point I allowed him an ironic smile and he said, 'She looks hammered.'

Her eye sockets had filled with dark pools of blood. He reached forward and dipped the end of his finger into one of the pools, like an inkwell, and painted the Star of David in blood on a box of Double Deckers next to her. 'They'll call it race-related now,' he said. 'And the press love a race-hate story.'

The next thing I knew there was a panicked hyperventilation going off behind me. I turned around.

'Hello,' he said. 'You must be Mother.'

First she saw the hammer in my hand, all bloody and black – sticky with clods of brain and hair, ripped and matted – and then she saw her daughter, upside down, broken in a bloody mess on the floor, dead. Our eyes met for only an instance. She was about to pop. There was no time for pleasantries or absurd dramatic dialogue. I swung the hammer and caught her full toss on her right temple. She went down quiet but it wasn't over. She was wriggling, holding her hands to her head and moaning. I stepped over her, raised the hammer high, clasping it tight with both hands and then brought it smashing down into the back of her head with an absolute crushing and murderous fury. I think I might have roared. The hammer smashed through the top of her skull, ripped through her brains, and embedded itself into the top of her spine. Her head was in two, torn apart like a hacked-in-half coconut. It was done. And she was dead. And that was that. It wasn't a pretty sight. I wrenched the hammer back out of her and placed it on the counter on top of a pile of unsold *Daily Mails*… Job done.

He stole three packets of Superkings and a couple of scratchcards, Thunderballs… I don't know why he stole Superkings, I don't smoke Superkings. I left fingerprints everywhere, but as he said, 'What does it matter? You'll be dead before they catch you.'

I stepped out of the shop onto a quiet empty street and ambled home unnoticed. It was one of those beautiful evenings that hang still and silent. The trees full and frothy with blossom. If the truth be told, I felt… a little bit extra.

I gave the scratchcards and Superkings to a drunk on Mare

Street. He seemed appreciative and offered God's blessings.

When I got in the long arm was east and the short arm west. It all seemed clear. Write it down, he said – every dirty word, he said, the truth of it, the awful evil truth of it. I made a cup of the Earl and rolled a jazz.

It is now nearly midnight. Both arms up... And I am mashed... and yawning. Yawning to the point of dislocation... I have no conscience... I am to bed.

To bed, Crumb... bread crumb... to bed.

# TUESDAY

It's no use, I can't sleep – he won't let me. His mind is racing with fiendish notions and fizzing with evil intent. The time is south by north-east. I have done a terrible thing, an awful evil thing, and yet I feel nothing. I have no conscience… I am a murderer. He snickers at this last remark and says that, come Friday, that will be the least of it. God, what if that's true? He keeps replaying every gruesome moment of the Sudder Street scandal over and over in his mind. Not in a Dostoevsky way, all miserable and guilty, but more in a Channel Five Reality TV's '100 most violent criminal acts ever caught on camera' sort of way: in at number nineteen, a new entry – fresh CCTV footage of a man who's clearly not happy with the service. We call it – Hammer Horror…

He's sitting in the kitchen now doing one of his drawings. He says we shouldn't waste time sleeping. 'Six days!' he keeps bellowing. 'Only six days left!' He says we should go immediately to the Shacklewell Lane and get a whore and anally rape her. I don't know that I can be arsed. That's my trouble, I can never really be bothered with any of it. Life, gnawing away at me, urging me on… I just can't be bothered. Take my teeth and leave me alone – I refuse to bite.

But it's no use – he's insisting on it – and he's got a point. If not now, when?

He got out of bed, pulled on his boots, threw on a coat and trudged the Downs to the Shacklewell Lane in search of some lickerish and a woman of shame.

The night was like a bottle of Verdicchio – cold, crisp, clean and moist. The wind whispering warnings and a light spit threatening reprisals. I arrived on the Shacklewell to find it deserted, not a soul in sight. Good, I thought – let's go home, get back into bed, snuggle up tight and appease yourself with a wank. But no, he said – 'Your blood's up,' he said. 'You've got the horn,' he said. 'There'll be no shillying out of it now,' he said – 'Oh no…' I sat down on the low wall outside the Texaco garage and waited, had a smoke and reflected… I hate episodes like this, I thought, the awful grubby reality of them.

'You can do all the talking,' I said. 'I'm staying out of it.'

'Fine,' he said. 'Good. The whole thing will be much more enjoyable without your meddling rectitude.'

'Fine,' I said. 'Good.' And fell silent.

I didn't have to wait long. After a minute or two a long thin Rastafarian gentleman materialized from nowhere, approached me and asked in a slow sonorous gnarl, 'Wat you wan?'

'I'm looking to rip the arse out of a whore,' he casually announced, carrying on like the Duke of Edinburgh. The Rastaman looked at me, pausing for a moment and then said, 'You want girl?'

'Yees – that's right,' he said, acting like a fifteen-year-old

Terry -Thomas on a weekend exeat in Amsterdam. It was embarrassing.

The Rastaman considered me, and then said, 'You sit on waall – one come along now.'

I sat back down on 'waall' and waited. Waited to see what obscene abomination would appear, and I didn't have to wait long. At first, from a distance, half-hidden in the shadows, she appeared to be quite attractive. She was jiggling lickety-split towards me, a pert forward quickstep and that good old-fashioned wiggle, wiggle. She was wearing a short denim skirt and jacket. Her figure was defined, thin and angular. Her limbs long. Over her right arm she carried a small fake Burberry handbag; and in her left hand she carried a half-eaten packet of Walkers crisps. As she grew closer her pace slowed to a cautious lope. She stopped. The Rastaman turned and looked at me.

'Dis girl,' he said, just in case I hadn't realized. I got up and approached the goods for closer inspection. And oh my God, what a raddled old skank cracker she was. Not at all the back-lit beauty of the shadows that I had imagined her to be as she gambolled from the darkness towards me – oh no. What in silhouette had seemed one thing, close up was quite another. Her naked greasy legs were covered in a violent camouflage of cuts and sores and track marks. Small dark thumb-sized bruises were dotted over her mauled, pawed and fingered flesh. Her skirt and jacket were old and out of fashion and stained and threadbare and worn. A dismal, emaciated, grizzled horror. She was wretched. And her face, dear God – the greatest horror of all – just recalling it makes me gag. She was probably about twenty-five but looked at least forty-five. Her skin was dead and rotting on the bone. It looked like the congealed fat in a frying pan after a greasy breakfast fry-up. Cratered with black scabs and heaving yellow spots, criss-crossed with a network of fine worn lines, and all of this bloated pustulating hideosity made garishly worse by the cheap liberal application of oily make-up. Her eyes were darting, hollow and empty, her expression haggard, cold, wary, hard and insolent, her mouth pulled sideways and down in a fixed rictus of devious suspicion. She was truly and utterly repulsive. Utterly disgusting. A heinous raddled whore of the lowest order. A common brown-road trollop. Crack-deformed skank, out of her mind, posturing on the pavement and wiggling her arse at the passing traffic. Fair enough, I thought. You've got to put your goods in the window.

'Is you looking for some bizniz?' she asked, her voice a coy paranoid jitter.

'Yes, I am,' he boldly replied, far too boldly in my opinion – over-compensating, trying to show everyone how at ease he was with the situation and not at all nervous. The fraud. She saw through him straight away. She thought he was a joke – and he knew it, which enraged him and delighted me.

'I want to storm the last bastion of your nakedness,' he went on, comically licking his lips.

'What?' she pecked, his literary allusions lost on her.

'I want to fuck you up the arse.'

'Oh, I fought you said you wanid ado somfin to me.'

'I do. I want to fuck you up the arse.'

The Rastaman looked at her, nodded downwards, then looked at me, jutted his chin forward, nodded upwards and said, 'You go wid 'er.'

'Is gonna cost ya,' she sniped in.

'Of course, my child.' I cannot believe he called her 'my child' – the shamefaced temerity! Heaping disgrace upon shame at every twist and turn – and she doesn't even realize it. 'How much?'

She didn't answer. Her eyes were darting suspiciously, there was a pause and everyone suddenly seemed unsure.

''Ere, you got a car?' she asked.

'No,' I said.

'Oh…' she said.

The management intervened, working the angles. 'Is gonna cost more widout a car.'

'Yeah,' she said, quickly taking up his lead. 'If you 'aven't got a car is gonna cost more if we have to go up vair.'

'How much more?' I was becoming slightly irritated.

'To fuck me in the arse?'

'To fuck you *up* the arse – yes.'

She paused. I waited. She was wondering how much she could take me for.

'Twenty pound.'

'Fine,' I said and handed her a crisp clean twenty-pound note. 'If you act like you're enjoying it, I'll tip you an extra tenner.'

That brought a smile to her face, which was an error on her part as it showed her teeth, or what was left of them. Dark rotten tarnished yellow stumps coated in the half-chewed remains of Walkers finest cheese-and-onion. I think I may have winced.

'Come on ven,' she said, and intertwined her arm through mine and led me up the street. I allowed her this intimacy for a step or two but then shrugged her off and told her not to walk so close. She didn't seem offended, but to be honest I didn't care – she stank. A pungent acid chemical stink, mixed with BO and vinegared crisps. Notably odious. We continued up the street for about twenty yards and then stopped next to a deep double doorway floodlit beneath an arc lamp. She turned her back to me and started lifting her skirt.

'Here?' I said, a little perturbed.

'Yeah – woss wrong wiv 'ere?'

'Everyone can see us.'

'So?'

'Can't we go somewhere a little more… shadowy?'

'I'm not doin nothin' funny. I dunno who you are. I'm not going in up an alley – an inyway vair ain't iny. You might wanta kill me.'

'I don't want to kill you – I want to fuck you up the arse.'

'All right – you dun arf go on a-bow-tit.' She pulled her skirt back down and continued on up the street. I followed. We turned into the Estate and crossed into an open stairwell. 'Happy now?' she said. 'Shadowy enough?' We were standing in a refuse stairwell surrounded by eight-foot-high metal dustbins filled with the foulest stinking rotting filth imaginable. I was gagging, ready to vomit. There were rats casually dining. And for this you pay extra?

'Are you ready ven?' she leered, reaching towards me and groping my crotch.

'No, I'm not,' I replied, unzipping my flies and removing my flaccid little spigot. Without hesitation she dropped to a squat and stuck her mouth on me, sucking and licking my tired limp and dirty little dick, urgently polishing me off. I looked mournfully down at her, yanking and twiddling, desperately trying to suck me into an erection. What a pity, I thought, what sad indignity is this – human beings, aren't they revolting? And to think how encrusted with dry piss and smegma my cock was. I could smell it. It stank. I thought I was going to throw up all over her. Shouldn't she have sheathed me, I thought? There's a procedure usually followed in these situations. This old strumpet's long since abandoned any codes of conduct. Hey ho, I thought, it's her look out. She's probably already diseased and past caring. Trying to spread it, I wouldn't wonder – her revenge on mankind. After about a minute she stood up, lit a cigarette, hitched her skirt up around her waist, turned to face the wall, spread her arms out in front of her, shoved her naked arse towards me and said, 'Go on ven, get on wiv it.' My cock was barely erect. Her arse was bruised, scratched and smeared with … God only knows what. It looked like dried blood, or dry shit. There were no buttocks to speak of – nothing to pinch or tweak or slap, nothing to plunder, no fat to cushion the pushing, as they say – just an angular arrangement of bones beneath worn stretches of yellow stained skin, divided down the middle by a dark dirty crack. The grotesque unwashed seedy reality of it all was working a wonder on my erection. The back-alley awfulness of it all was far more arousing than the sex of it. I reached forward and peeled her arse open. Her sphincter was a slack gaping hole. It's fair to say I wasn't her first. I looked to the night sky and the stars and then drove my cock into her in one smooth determined stroke. She didn't even notice. I stabbed away at her, jabbing it in and out, grunting and puffing – harder and harder, my pelvis impacting into her with increasing malice and resentment, my fingers gripping her bony hips, clawing into her, tearing her arse apart, wanting to hurt her – but all to no avail – the fucking trollop paid no attention at all, just kept sucking on her fag and spitting. You could have fucked her with a twelve-inch carving knife and she wouldn't have noticed. My pace and vigour ensured it didn't last long. I squirted a little blob, grunted and was done. She pulled her skirt down, and turned to face me, her fag dangling between her teeth.

'Dat was nice,' she said, angling for her extra tenner.

I ignored her, pushed my cock into my trousers and fumbled up my flies. She looked so pathetic and hopeless. So utterly fucked-up and debased. She was just a bit of rotten flesh, a skinny, crack-addled Hackney whore – to be used and done with in whatever scandalous or outrageous or offensive a way one wished. I actually felt a little sorry for her. What a monstrous ghastly frightful reality was hers.

'Why do you do this?' I asked.

She looked at me and smiled that coy, hideous derangement of features and said, 'Is the crack innit.'

'Why don't you get off it?' I earnestly went on. 'You're young still – you could get on a programme, start again. Clean yourself up – start over.' How foolish I must have sounded.

'First you do dat to my arse'ole and now you wanna save me?'

She had a point, but I didn't relent – the bit was between my teeth. 'Why not? You could – if you wanted. You can't do this, go on doing this – lifting your skirts for sick twisted perverts like me to stick their cocks up – for twenty pounds – to put in your pipe and smoke! Come on,' I went on, 'this life will kill you. Look at you – you're young. This doesn't need to be your life. Save yourself – before it's too late. Imagine a different life.'

She was staring at me, wide-eyed and bewildered. Confused but moved. This sort of post-coital intimacy was obviously alien to her. She didn't know how to respond.

'But…' she tentatively stammered.

'Go on,' I gently coaxed.

'Is the crack innit…'

What was the use, and what was I thinking – this gutter-snipe wretch had no capacity to imagine, no capacity to imagine anything, to imagine at all. Just a stupid human, a dullard like the rest, an ignorant dolt – slovenly, indulgent and useless. She enraged me. Stupid humans. My touchy-feely compassionate conservatism was rapidly giving way to something quite other. An acid spike of hatred was rushing through me. A bitter incensed resentment, curdling into violence.

'Are you laughing at me?' I suddenly barked, surprising myself as much as her. 'Don't think I don't know!'

She was wedged between a bin and the wall, staring at me. Her eyes flickering with fright, or flight, or fight. She knew well not to speak. There was something animal between us… I could feel my face peeling into convulsive cackles of sneering laughter: 'HAhahahahaha!!! HAhahahahaha!!! HAhahahaha-ha!!!'

The tart was looking very confused.

'Look at you,' I snapped. 'Look at you – you raddled fuck. Just a piece of cunt that I can do what I like with – aren't you? Look at you!? A slice of the pie to fuck and forget! And what's wrong with that, eh? What's not to like?! Look at you – in a dustbin, snivelling grubby reality. Grubby reality! I can smell it on you. Sucking cocks for fivers – that's your life! You'll be dead in week – dead in a week! They'll come knocking and you'll be rotting! Dead on the floor in a corner. Knickers round your ankles, arse in the air. Dead in a crack-hole cave. Dead. You'll be scraped up off the floor and shovelled into bin bags by a pair of underpaid council workers who'll grumble and moan about the stench of you even after you're dead. They'll sling you out with the rubbish and burn you up at the dump. And all will be pleased, and glad to see the back of you. And that will be that. No-one will miss you. No-one will remember you. It'll be as if you had never existed, and frankly, my dear, better if you hadn't!'

I grabbed her by the throat and pinned her pathetic frame against the wall. I pulled the extra tenner from my pocket, put my face close to hers and whispered, 'Daddy can't come on Thursday, but Mummy will kiss you good night.' And with that I reached for her face and stuffed the tenner into her mouth and forced it as far down her throat as I could push it. I released my grip. She fell to her knees, coughing and choking, clawing at her throat, gagging and retching. I took a step back away from her, giving myself some room, and then swung my leg and toe-punted her in the face. She reeled backwards, clattered against a bin and collapsed. Her two front teeth were broken and lying at right angles to her gums, blood and spit trickling

... She didn't move, but she wasn't dead. She made a small almost imperceptible 'umph' noise and then farted.

I knew this would happen... I should have stayed at home, I thought, and had that wank. Why did I listen to him? Look at her. Poor bloody wretch... Look what you've done to her.

I squatted beside her, reached into her mouth and pulled the tenner back out of her throat. Her Majesty was not amused. Darwin looked appalled.

'I'm sorry...'

She rolled away from me. It was strange, the way she rolled, the way she folded her arms into herself, the fall of her shoulder, and her sniffling tears, it all made me think of Valerie.

I don't know why I got into such a rage with her, but now I feel low and rotten and ashamed. And he did it to me! I am foul and loathsome and rotten and wrong. Wrong, I tell you! Wrong!

I am a man of evil conscience... And a man of evil conscience cannot act well...

It is late and I should to bed again and try and sleep. I have been awake for nearly twenty hours... I do have a conscience... I do.

I am going to bed. And I fully expect to suffer terrible nightmares.

Noon arms up, and in good spirits. Slept like a sloth – six pure hours of uninterrupted kip. I'm restored and there's a spring in my step, as they say. Got out of bed on the right side. Feet straight into my slippers. Everything in place, no trouble with my breathing. An honest and relaxed performance. Everything quite as it should be. Behaviour – daily to commonplace routine. Normal. All of last night's cares seem quite forgotten. I'm lifted. It is a new day. Tuesday.

I'm sat in Don's. I've just finished my eggs, scrambled this morning, and very nice they were too – consistent colouring throughout. Indulgent dollops of ketchup splashed all over. Yummy yummy. Sad reports on the wireless this morning. Videotapes have been released showing an Englishman chained in a cage, pleading for his life. The Arabs are going to cut his head off. The nation is outraged in a resigned-to-it 'poor bugger' sort of way. Timid English indignation – honestly, they couldn't give a tuppenny fuck really. But I digress. So much has happened since I woke I feel quite carried away by it all. Events – freak occurrences – things that happen – unexpected knockings on your door at nine-fifteen in the morning. Who could that be, he wondered?

I got up, shuffled down the corridor and peered through my spyhole – 'Well I never,' he said. 'The cleaning lady.' He invited her in, told her I had just made a pot of tea and showed her through into the living room, which was in a bit of a state but it didn't seem to faze her. He was right, by the way – she is Polish. Her name is Milka, I think – she said it very quickly and then didn't repeat it, it could have been Mirka but I think it was Milka. She very politely and courteously explained to me how she was going to each flat and handing out cards offering her services as a cleaner. She suggested coming two or three times a week in my case and then joked that I could 'use her'. He smiled at that. 'Has anyone taken you up on your offer?' he enquired – ever so politely, it surprised me. No, she replied, and shifted her weight and looked at her feet. I could tell she was embarrassed, ashamed of herself and the humiliating effort of life – so I cleared a seat for her and told her to sit down, and then went into the kitchen and poured her a nice hot cup of tea and brought it back out to her and sat down beside her and we had a very pleasant chat. She told me all about her husband Yaroslav and how he worked on a site in Whitechapel. How they'd come over from Warsaw two years ago and settled in Leyton. She spoke eloquently and ironically about how the business degree she'd graduated with in Poland was useless to her here, but that her formerly useless husband's skills as a plumber were in great demand. I told her how it was just me here now and that I probably could use some help around the house with some of the cleaning and a bit of ironing. I said I'd enjoy the company as much as anything – it'd be nice to have someone to talk to, I said, as I don't get out much. I know that's a lie, but lying is the common currency in any human exchange. She said she could start tomorrow and I said, 'Right, it's a date then.' We stood up and shook hands and smiled at each other properly, kindly, like two people. I said I'd see her in the morning and that I'd be looking forward to it. She said okay, and then off she went... She has got a lovely bottom.

I stood in the middle of the room smelling the remains of her scent in the air... Milka. What a delightful way to start the day. Like two people, it was very nice... I felt quite moved. The simple honest yak that strangers share, a cordial fumbling, an amiable getting-to-know. It was very nice. I felt quite overtaken by it all and went and soaked in a long hot bath and thought about her. Everything had kicked off on the right foot and nothing had gone wrong. I lay there and thought about her until the water turned tepid and my skin began to curl. He said she was ever so much cleaner close up, in real life as it were, than he had ever imagined her to be when he watched her through the spyhole. I agreed, she did look clean, and her skin was ever so white. As white as alabaster, he said. As white as milk, I say. Semi-skimmed Milka. She had such a light and delicate way about her too, a fragility that made you want to protect her. Yes. And a lovely bottom. She was a pretty all right, not a stupid. I gave myself a good lather, washed my pits and shaved my face, cleaned my teeth and combed my hair. Gave myself a good polish. And I polish up well I should tell you. As a young man I was very handsome. I bet you didn't expect that, did you? No, you probably think I'm a repugnant fiend with a hairy back, bulging warts and abnormally proportioned features and flat feet. Well, I'm not. Oh no – I'm handsome. Very handsome. A handsome youth, they used to say, when I was a boy. And I was. I turned heads, you know. Everywhere I went I was always looked at. The eyes have always been on me. Looking at me. I've grown used to it… Oh yes, I'm a head-turner all right – a handsome head-turner, that's what my mum used to call me… And looking at me now, in my old suit and tie, socks and shoes, I'd say I've still got it… should I want it. A little worn, perhaps, here and there, but nothing shameful. Greying at the temples. Frayed around the edges, perhaps – but characterful, I'd say, yes. A handsome melancholy fellow. Yes. Handsome and melancholy, but with a spring in his step this morning. Milka. She has affected me. But I digress. She does have a lovely bottom.

Another episode of note this morning was my stool. Much improved on yesterday's – Grade 3 on the Bristol this morning: 'Sausage with cracked surface'. (Possible title for my memoirs?)

I'm leaving Don's now to go and meet a man called Dieter. Dieter is German and sells drugs. I have 'known' him for many years. Once a month I buy an ounce of hashish from him. Today I will buy something altogether stronger. The headline in the paper this morning read:

# MY DRUGS SHAME

I think we're going to have fun.

North, south-east.

I am not myself. I am drugged, addled, and split. My mind is in pieces. Shattered, I tell you – shattered! I'm transmuted. My thinking is out of all control. I am profoundly confused. My heart is beating and then not beating. My breathing is backward. Total derangement. Rabid uncertainty. Dread behind, panic before. Fear. Uncertainty. And danger. Find the start. Begin again. Order your thoughts. Where were you? At Don's. You left Don's. Yes – I left Don's. What was the headline? The headline! Yes – that's right, I went to Dieter's – yes, that's right. Both arms up, eggs scrambled, newspaper, headline. You're guessing. I can't remember. This is terrible. Time has gone haywire. A tempest of remembrance raging unchecked without any consideration for the thinker. I am drugged. Drugged, I tell you! Drugged! I'm unhinged! And have been for some time. I cannot be certain of specifics, and will make no sense trying to. I can smell damp. It smells familiar. Dieter answered the door. Yes – he was wearing a dhoti – that's right, a lungi – yes, a kikoi – that's right, yes, a sarong – remember? Naked, but for all else other than only in a dhoti! And the sweet stench of incense – immediately and all consumingly soaking into me, remember? You said to remember for later thinking that you were feeling infected – it infecting you – do you remember? Stinking of it, you said – and that strange tribal music too, playing low in the background, crawling underneath, texturing the silence – d'you remember? Subverting the surroundings, you said – remember? Remember that for later, you said. Yes, and everything was red. Red – that's right. Everything was red – and flaming. Burning. A swirling inferno.

Licking every inch of her. Remember. Her hair. Smouldering red against pale skin. The ends of you split. Writhing. Remember? It was a long time ago, I concede, but nevertheless. That searing heat. You weren't much older than a lad. A ruddy youth – red in the cheeks with the first flush of love – scuffling along in your Sunday best. I'll never forget her – pretty in a springtime dress. Proud and haughty in a pair of muddy gumboots, with her wild red hair billowing all about her, burning the air around her. Joking and teasing and laughing. Days to remember, those, and with fondness recall. Yes – the comfort of each other, so at ease, walking and talking and teasing and laughing. How many happy afternoons did we giggle on the swings. Two exhausted children, panting and smiling. The gentle riffle of the wind between leaves, and the quiet ache of her branches. I was so happy, and so in love. I thought those days would never end. I wanted to hold you, and kiss you, and tell you that I loved you. But I didn't. I mumbled and nodded and looked at my feet. A callow youth, embarrassed by his need for another. And then you said you were leaving. My heart was bursting. It couldn't be. Those last cracked kisses, your broken blistered lips, goodbyes whispered, and tears sent to circle... I carved your name next to mine in the sycamore bark. I remember my knife catching and the blade snapping and my hand bleeding... All the tears that I shed for you, caught in a bloody palm... I loved you...

Dear God, what's happening to me? My memory is jumping and carnivalling all over, darting off and beginning again – it's all I can hope for it to end. Bombarded with thoughts, jockeying and jostling – everything wrong and off at a kilter – the endless bits of forgotten in-between returning to haunt me – it's a madness uncontrolled! That bastard Dieter. What has he done to me? You asked for it, mate. And paid for it. Put one before the other and begin. You know this. You'll be fine.

'Petta Krum… Ve meet again.'

His hazy delivery of the simplest sentence – d'you remember? – you said he's totally stoned. And paranoid. Look at him, you said – remember? When he didn't quite hear you, and looked at you in that way that you didn't understand, and there was a breath of something between you, for less than a second – remember? I'm a customer, not a friend, you said. That's right, and he was totally stoned. Don't get me wrong, you said, I like Dieter, you said, he's reliably detached, you said, won't ask questions of any depth, you said – remember? He'll make statements, parrot truisms and tell anecdotes, but that's all. You like it that way. I do. He doesn't want your friendship or your kinship, no, he wants my money… Yes, and I want his drugs.

'Vat vill it be today, Petta?' I hate the way he calls me 'Petta'.

'Your usual lump of London soap?' Too much sneer, I remember that. 'Or perhaps a little something stronger?' That's where it all went wrong. He always offers something a little stronger, but I never accept. I'm a lump-of-London-soap man. Always have been. He holds me in contempt for this, of course he does, he looks down on me as a poor customer, yes, that's the truth of it – he despises me my moderation. I'm a poor return and he knows it. What did he give me? That vicious bastard. What have I taken? How long will this last? What did I say to him – think – think clearly – go back, see it, picture it… Red, moaning, beads, stink, tribal. I think I was sitting – what did I say? You said – of course –

'Actually, Dieter, I am looking for something altogether stronger.'

That's right. Remember his eyes? They lit up. He looked interested, didn't he? Interested in you. A spring in your step and he noticed. It's Tuesday, you said. Six days left and then you're dead – remember? Remember the whore? That dirty old sumka with her broken teeth. Irrational bloody babbling. I can't stop exercising my jaw – obsessively shifting it, right and left, like a bloody camel. I seem to remember doing this on a bus and being looked at by disapproving women. Was that today? I have no recollection of leaving Dieter's and getting home. What time is it? East, south-east. There are three hours unaccounted for. What did he do to me? You were lying comatose on the carpet. What? Dieter had been through your pockets and robbed you. What? Nothing would revive you. What are you talking about? You can't recall? He kept calling your name. Yes, I remember – it was my father. He was calling me. I remember hearing my father as the reflection of the voice of God, as a human faculty, calling me, Peter, Peter. I was looking at my coins upstairs in my bedroom. D'you remember? Those coins you kept. Your collection. Remember those coins? You loved your coins. That special big one from the Jubilee. And that one with David Platt from the box of Shreddies. D'you remember? Dad was calling you down for your dinner and you were looking at your coins. Remember? They weren't my coins. You didn't collect coins, it wasn't me. You're very confused.

They were Emma's coins. Remember? Emma's coin collection. She did a project for school. You were her father. It was you calling. It was you calling. Lying on the floor, a grown man, out of his mind, calling out for Daddy. Aren't you ashamed? I'm exhausted. I need to rest. You're always resting. Forever tired. No, I'm not. Yesterday you said you suffered permanent feelings of tiredness. No, I didn't. Yes, you did. You said that's as maybe. What? Exactly – you can't hijack me with your syntax and tenses. I'm not German!

'Vat are you after, Petta?'

'My drugs shame.' That's right. That's it – 'My drugs shame.' Well, you found it all right.

He led you down a corridor and into the sitting room – that's how it was. Everything was red, and stinking of incense, there was a tribal moaning. You took a seat on the sofa – yes, that's right – it was an orange sofa, not red. The walls were red or the light was red, it was dark, the curtains – not curtains, a blind – that's right, yes – a blanket nailed over the window – yes... He draped himself on the floor in front of you next to a low glass coffee table – didn't he? Yes, and his cock fell out and he took rather too long to put it away, didn't he? – that's right. Why do you remember that? There was a large purple bong. The water pipe – remember? – tarnished and stained. Many hours smoking and glorious boom shanking. Did he say that? There were some scales, I think. Is that right? He saw me looking at the bong, didn't he, and he offered it – that's right. Remember, he said, 'You vanna smoke a bong?' And then he immediately set about burning lumps, and crumbling and packing. What the hell did he put in it?

'Vat kind of shame you looking for, Petta?'

'Whatever shame you got, Dieter.' I remember saying that.

'Shame can cost a lot of money Petta.' Twiddling his beads. Fingering suspicion, burning lumps and crumbling powders. Shifty, you said – remember? – the way he twiddles his beads – shifty, you said, see how shifty he is. Remember? He was eyeing you. Twiddling suspicion, and eyeing you.

'You looking very smart today, Petta, you got a court appearance?'

My suit, of course, he saw me polished. That's right – he was suspicious because I was wearing a suit, with socks and shoes. That's right. Polished – remember?

'First ve smoke a bong, Petta, then ve put our minds to something special, yah?'

Yah... yah... yah... Hubble bubble, hubble bubble.

What did he put in that pipe? God only knows. A mixture of all sorts. A little bit of everything – some crack, some smack, a little bit of DMT. The front of my face feels... It's hard to explain and will make no sense, but the front of my face feels – ajar. And numb. And an incredible hum is radiating outwards from the middle of my brain and pulsing against the inside of my skull, reverberating and echoing back in on itself. All sound is heightened, layered, simple, perfect, and acute. I can hear everything as far away as Rendlesham Road. I have become an ear – I *am* an ear – listening and vibrating at a very low frequency. There is a continual adjustment in the lighting and, as I said, time is all over the place – I have no sense of it. I noted that down somewhere, mentally noted it down for later. Yes. And I thanked you for it too. Good for you, I said. Get stuck in,

I said. I'm no man's fool, you said. I didn't know what you were talking about. You took the bong and the next thing I knew you were rolling your eyeballs and trying to swallow my tongue. Remember? You jumped up, wobbled, and said you had to leave, then you looked at your watch, asked what time it was and sat down again, held your head for a moment and then stood up again and said you were going to throw up. You staggered four paces, stopped, wobbled, looked giddy, lurched for the door frame and collapsed... It was hilarious. Puff Puff Puff! Swallowing huge plumes of purple haze. Then down you go – gurgling, swallowing your tongue, jerking and slathering like a slaughtered goat! A complete fucking spectacle you made of yourself. It was hilarious! I was laughing my head off. I nearly choked.

Dieter showed no mind of course. He's seen it all before, simply got up and made himself a cup of tea. Came back ten minutes later to check on you, slumped on the floor with your arse in the air, totally comatose. He rolled you over and pulled you straight, remember?... Oh God. He did something, didn't he? I knew it.

'You looking for some shame, Petta? You looking for some shame, Petta Krum?'

Oh my God... He fiddled with my trousers, didn't he?

'I'll show you some shame, Petta Krum.'

I remember thinking at the time that someone was fiddling with my trousers. I thought it was you. But it wasn't. It was him.

I knew it. I knew it then too. He's fiddling with my trousers – I can remember thinking it. It was like a dream. I felt so heavy. It was impossible to move. He pulled my trousers down and he put something up me. Oh dear God – he raped me! No. No, he didn't. He didn't. He put his fingers up me. Yes, that's what he did. He stuffed something up me. Oh dear God. What did he stuff up me?

OPIUM. Opium. Oh thank God. It's the opium. That's where I am. Opium. Opium. Oh the relief. The blessed relief. Now I know where I am. I'm on opium. Oh thank Christ. It's only the O. That bugger Dieter. Honestly. Oh thank Christ. I know where I'm up to. Yes… Yes, that's right – 'I'll show you some shame, Petta Krum.' Yes – what else was there? Some cocaine, I seem to recall. Yes, I did a line of charlie, didn't I? I can recall the preparation note-rolling and afterwards nostril-burning… yes… And then that's when I realized. That's when I realized it wasn't cocaine, do you remember? It was ketamine! You fool! That came as a surprise to you, didn't it? Great fat line of it. Chop chop chop. Two inches long and half an inch thick. Little bit of a livener, you said. One for the road, you said. Get me back on my feet before I leave, you said.

'Go for it!' he said. 'Yah – go crazy, Krum. Let yourself go.'

Remember? One for the road all right, wasn't it? And into the K-hole hell you fell. Hahahahahah! Please stop… Please. I feel very other. I am not myself. I feel very unfamiliar. There's a lump of opium up your arse and a horse tranquillizer coursing through your brain – what do you expect? Hahahahah!

Between leaving Dieter's and getting home, I cannot recall … There are three hours I cannot account for. Where have I been? What have I done? My jacket is on the floor. There is a dark oily stain I don't recognize…

I think I…

North and south.

Have had a bit of a disco nap, and am feeling a little more composed, but am still quite deranged. I have had another line of ketamine, I found a whole wrap of it in my sock, and I'm getting a second wind. I'm feeling fruity and thinking of going out.

Short south-west, long north-north-east.

Quiet in a corner of the Coach and Horses, stewing my tits off, a wonderful warm glow all about me – mulled and calm and sitting comfortably, contented and ready to begin. But first you must indulge my digression. I want to tell you about a man called David Cornell. David Cornell was a friend of mine – well, not so much a friend exactly, more of a 'colleague', we worked together many years ago, he'd be long since forgotten were it not for memory. Dave was managerial material from the moment you met him. Slacks from his hips to his ankles and never a crease where there wasn't a pleat. Popular too. Very able. A safe pair of hands, as they say. Qualified and accomplished. Good with the rank and file... Something of a cunt, I always thought, but like everybody else I anxiously sought his approval. What a timid little villain I was. I thought he was better than me, you see. A better man than me. More than me. He had a group, you see – a clique. They were the envy of the whole department. Dave's gang. I bitterly resented them, begrudged them their union – but pathetically sought their endorsement. Peevish little squealer that I was – needing confirmation. A scampering creep, that's what I was, but they were sharp and brash and confident, and seemed to have a monopoly on happiness and fun. Always having it, they were – fun. Having fun and being happy. They made me sick. They would all go out together after work and drink and smoke and lech and snipe and ridicule and mock and gossip and lie and say clever things and laugh. They would meet others who in their turn would drink and smoke and lech and snipe and ridicule and mock and gossip and lie and say clever things and laugh. They would pull drunken gutter tarts in a hope to impress, high on a bottle of the dogs, and drag them home and spread them out for a lonely late-night filth-time fuck. And the next day report back to their master Dave the night before's rotten remembered antics.

I grew bored of Dave Cornell and his miserable little world of saying clever things and laughing. His noxious personality, that he spent so long styling, and his poisonous entourage of lickspittle phonies. The smug attendants of his court. The lot of them made me sick – literally sick – bucketfuls of half-digested slop thrown up out of sheer fear every morning before entering the office. I remember I withdrew further and further into my corner and said nothing. Keep your mouth shut, I said. Be silent, I said. Give nothing away. Hope they don't notice. Afraid to be met, seen or spoken to. The dread of being spoken to, and having to justify myself – urgh. I can feel it again now as I think about it. Explaining myself away. It's all I've ever engaged in. Private consultations with myself from the moment I wake and all through my sleep – justifying, rationalizing, vindicating myself – driving myself out of my mind with it. I remember it exhausted me then too. And left me ailing. I despised them all. And feared them all. Kept myself to myself and refused to engage. They didn't like that. They didn't like that one bit. My fear and hatred festered and grew until I could take it no more. It was at this time that I first started scratching my ankle. Yes, that's when the itching started. And the yearning.

They scoffed when I told them I was leaving. Openly laughed in my face. Treated me with utter contempt. 'Off to write your opus, Crumb?' Snickering up their sleeves at me. Eyes behind my back at me. Razzing me. Teasing me. The ridicule I endured. They wanted me dead. Ignorant dolts, parasitic whistlers, saying clever things and laughing.

I mention this now because David Cornell is standing at the bar. He's fatter than he was and drinking Guinness. He hasn't seen me yet, but he will. I wonder will he recognize me? You're polished – he's bound to. He's getting a round in. Always very generous. Who's he with?… Of course, the cocaine rats – Paul and Dan. Two grovelling little nose-beggars, pet snivellers and resident jesters – still after all of these years with their fingers in his wallet and their tongues down the back of his Farah trousers. Pathetic eager acolytes – weak… and old now, look at them. Paul looks bizarre. He was always oddly proportioned, gorilla's arms on a donkey's frame with a gudgeon's head. And now he's bald and wearing cowboy boots. What a cunt. Dan's head looks like an old mangelwurzel – red and green and tuberous. And enormous – far too large for his frame, has his body shrunk? His face looks like it's melting. What are they laughing about? What have they got to be so amused by? Look at them. Bastard grunts. Why don't they notice me?

Dave just looked straight at me and walked right past me. I held his eye for quite a bit more than a moment but he just looked straight through me – didn't recognize me at all. His face was bloated. He's lost his looks all right. And so fat. An enormous gut – my God what a gut! I hate fat people. They disgust me. Look at him, sat there, with his pint of brown. Proud fat King Cornell. The mean vulgarity of the man. He's handing a wrap of cocaine to Dan under the table. Having a night out, boys? Wankers. Paul and Dan waste no time and scuttle to the bogs to powder their noses and finger each other's arses. This is my moment. He's alone. I'm going to join him.

As I approached his tiny pig eyes were on me. Beadying me up and down. I stopped about two feet from him and peered at him and said, very sanely and realistically, 'Dave? David Cornell? Is that you? Good Lord.'

His fat lips, like two over-ripe segments of orange, peeled forward into an open hole. 'Do I know you?' he drawled. His voice as fat and as glutinous as the rest of him, syrupy and slow with an awful nasal twang for added repugnance.

'It's Peter. Peter Crumb. We used to work together at – '

'Oh I remember you…' he sneered, interrupting, glancing twelve and six, taking in the length of me.'Yeah…. Didn't you go mental?'

I looked abashed, smiling coyly and then trying to sound impressive said – 'Yes, I left to write a book.'

'Oh, right – yeah,' he said in the language of a slovenly informalist. He couldn't give a toss. He wanted me to piss off. I extended my hand cordially towards him. He looked uncertain for a moment, demeaned, unsure of what to do. I held my ground, smiling at him in that imbecilic way that humans do, until he at last reluctantly took my hand, wrapping his fat fingers around mine like a half a dozen Cumberlands splitting beneath the grill.

'Well, it's good to see you again,' he said with a goodbye-and-now-please-leave curtness.

'Yes. It's been a long time,' I replied, sitting down next to him and spreading myself out. 'So, what are you up to these days?' I was imperious. As confident as a cabinet minister.

He eyed me suspiciously. 'I've set up on my own now,' he said, proudly reclaiming some status. 'Last seven years in fact. Couldn't be doin' better.'

'Still out whoring on a Tuesday though, eh?' I said, snorting like a fool and patting his shoulder. He didn't appreciate that.

He grunted with pretend amusement and looked around for the Toilet Two. I took a sup on my pint and paused, feeling pleased with myself. It was a mistake. In that moment of silence, in that instant of present time between past and future, all assurance and certitude left me. And a sudden spasmodic wave of derangement came over me as I remembered what condition I was in – what was up me and in me – the O and K. A hot flush of fear ran down my spine and all my confidence drained from me. He was looking at me, at my shabby attire, my cheap old suit, the stain I can't explain, the frayed edges and the broken time-worn failed greyness of me. I suddenly felt so ashamed and hostile. I angrily relit my rollie and looked randomly around the room, my disposition transforming into frightened obeisance. He'd seen through me in an instant. I was making a fool of myself and he knew it – which made it all the worse. I felt a crashing fear and terrible anxiety suddenly invade me. An awful cold dread and paranoid panic. I wanted to get up and leave but I couldn't. Dan and Paul were returning from the toilet, sniffing, grinning and trying to sparkle.

'Who's this then?' said Dan.

'I remember you,' said Paul, putting his hand on my shoulder.

'It's Peter,' Dave interjected.

'Peter Crumb – fuckin' hell.'

'I remember you.'

'Long time no see.'

'Peter fucking Crumb...'

And then there was a silence. It was excruciating. I couldn't think of anything to say. My mind straining like a screaming stuck cog, ripping itself apart. I sat there staring at them. My face paralysed into a contorted twitching palsy, sweat leaking out of me from every pore, burning and staining me. I tried to smile, approximated a laughing sound and took a long slug on my beer, spilling it all down the front of me.

'Didn't you go mental or somefin?'

'Now now, Dan, be nice,' said Dave, as if talking to a ten-year-old. 'Peter left to write a book. Didn't you, Peter?'

'Yees,' I said, trying to sound sage and ironic.

Paul laughed. 'Sold the movie rights yet?'

Dan started cackling, and Dave joined in. They thought I was a prat. The swines, openly laughing in my face.

'I didn't ever write it,' I blurted proudly.

'Why's that then – couldn't find your crayons?'

Their faces were creasing and juddering, cackling gales of scorn. I held myself perfectly still, smiling at them. You can't hurt me, I kept saying to myself – you can't hurt me any more, I've been around the block, I've seen the sights. What the fuck do you know? There was a fork on the table which I contemplated grabbing and stabbing into the back of Paul's hand but I showed restraint. Rather dignified, I thought, for a man in my condition.

'I got married,' I said. 'And had children… Had a child…'

'Really?' said Dan – looking to Dave to say something clever.

'It didn't work out,' I went on. 'You may have read something about it in the newspapers. It wasn't on the television.'

They didn't know what I was talking about – all three just looked at me, their faces fixed, bored with derision and amused confusion. Paul looked at Dan, Dan looked at Dave, Dave raised his eyebrows. Dan pulled the sides of his mouth down. Paul scrunched his nose. I raised my left eyebrow and lowered my right eyelid and pushed my tongue into my cheek. I don't know why I pulled such an odd expression. My face just sort of contorted into it. A strange, winking, tongue-in-cheek, postmodern derangement that I held for some time. Dave, Dan, and Paul all looking at me as though I were mad. As well they might.

'You feeling all right, Crumb?'

'D'you think I'm some sort of class spastic?' I suddenly spat, pushing my face forward into Dave's.

'What?'

'Easy, mate.'

'Don't get out ya pram.'

'No-one said you was a spastic.'

'He's just havin a laugh, en 'e?'

'We used to work together,' I hissed, as though that meant something.

'Yeah?' said Dave. 'So what?'

'I left that dump years ago,' said Paul

'Full of fuckin' monkeys that place,' said Dan.

And they all three stared at me, snarling, ready to bite.

'What are you doin' 'ere anyway, Crumb?'

'Yeah, what do you want, Crumb?'

'Why don't you sling it, mate.'

'Yeah – go on, fuckin' hop it.'

They really couldn't have made their position on my presence any clearer. I was about to tamely retire and shuffle off when fate stepped in and the devil closed ranks... At that moment three girls arrived and everything changed. Everything was suddenly diffused and different. The girls belonged to Dave. They made straight for him and festooned him in a wild flurry of kisses. A mad rash of lips and cheek perfumed the air. Short skirts on nimble frames with naked legs danced the awkward round of Hi and Nice to meet you. Kirsten, Kate and Kim. Hoorah, the boys shouted, the girls have arrived, hissing and scratching with kisses and smiles. Drinks were bought and coats removed, chairs found and arses parked. I was ignored throughout. So, I thought, everyone now seated – we will begin again.

'My name's Peter,' I announced to the girls like some Special Needs tit. They all six of them looked at me. I just wanted one of them to smile. To be kind and show favour. But they didn't. The girls were completely indifferent to me. They smelt me out as a wrong 'un straight away. My handsome melancholy demeanour meant nothing to this crowd. I was shut out and ignored, locked away at the awkward end of the table, stuck behind and in between, all backs opposing, everybody determined to have absolutely nothing to do with me. I sat there rejected, listening to their hateful emptiness. Their mournfully gormless opinions. Their witless regurgitations and vain observations. Their barbarous ignorance. The brash, loud-mouthed, unembarrassed, simple-minded twerpery of them. I was biting the edge of my glass listening to them. Every now and again I would throw in a little something to tease their blinkered view, but all to no avail. They'd look at me for a moment and either say nothing or go 'Right, yeah,' and then laugh and disparage and mutter curses.

The girls were particularly woeful. Craven leeches, auditioning for the role of tonight's slut. Eyeing each other all over – sizing themselves up against one another, wondering who would get who? One of them, the Kirsten one, kept stealing glances my way. She was ugly but thought she was beautiful, and would be thought of by others as beautiful too, but she's an ugly all right. Ugly in every way. Selfish, thick, deluded, greedy and vain. I heard her ask Dave who 'that weirdo' was. She was referring to me. Dave told her I was 'some twat' he used to work with. He pointedly said it loud enough for me to hear. I raised my empty pint pot and said cheers. Everybody laughed at that.

The other girl, the Kate one, was even more repugnant, oozing a sort of cheap pretend whoredom – a 'come and kiss me if you're hard enough' vapidity that she thought makes her alluring, dominant and modern. A stuck-up sex tramp in slingbacks and second-hand Gucci. A sorry little princess must-have with her flaccid tits on the table, dribbling sad stories about mummy and daddy's divorce and how neither of them wanted her...

The third, the Kim girl, was a say-nothing, sip-and-smoke type. Underwired and waxed, with a bum-fluff bleached moustache. Too feeble-minded to think or speak. Shallow, preening, vacant fuckbags – all three. They'll be getting it good and proper tonight. Given it every which way. All of this aren't we special – look at me – touch my tits – aren't I clever – pinch my arse – lick my finger and spunk on my face gentility. Who do they think they are? The middle classes and their damned liberality. Have another Breezer, girls, and get that up your nose. Everything is permitted but nothing is true. It's enough to make you want to convert to Islam. Wretched infected animals – freedom's monkey slaves!

I shuffled to the bar and bought another pint and a couple of rum chasers. When I returned to the table they had all closed ranks and spread themselves out, making it impossible for me to rejoin them. Pathetic and petty, I thought, but I wasn't bothered, I didn't want to sit with them anyway. I sat at the next table, feet away from theirs, meekly by myself. Humiliated, scorned and bereft. Slighted by everybody. The never-ending unbearable humiliation of it all. I was feeling so zonked and abstract. I just sat there lost, stuck in a state of staring. Feeling very odd. They ignored me, drinking and chatting, saying clever things and laughing. Occasionally one of them would glance my way and snicker and make a comment. Occasionally I would glance their way and laugh ridiculously loudly. 'Very droll – hahahhah – yes, very clever,' I barked at random intervals. My eyelids glowering. I was so pissed and stoned. I was making a complete fool of myself. Oh Crumb.

As the hours passed I felt more and more morbid and forlorn and floppy. Why are you doing this? I asked myself. Because the paper said so, came his predictable reply. It wasn't much of a consolation. This is your drug shame, Peter – this is life in the fast lane, mate, twenty-first century – you're cutting the edge of modernity here, my friend. Sharpening your wits with the in-crowd. You're the manifestation of the times in which we live, Peter. Think about it. I couldn't be bothered to think about it. I didn't know what I was talking about. Drug-induced drivelling babble it sounded like to me. Reported received regurgitated and replayed. An endless series of tor-ments, crushing humiliations and attacks of spleen. Alone, frightened, dirty and full of shame. And bursting for a piss.

Dave and Paul were scampering off to the khazi. I shuffled in after them and drained a gallon of urine into the bowl and all over the floor. I could hear Paul and Dan in the cubicle doing their business. I waited for them to re-emerge. The cubi-cle door opened and they both stepped out, sniffing and gurn-ing. I stepped in front of them and asked, 'Could I have some of that?'

'Some of what?' said Paul.

'Some of that cocaine you've been snorting.'

'Fuck off, Crumb, you twat.' Dan pushed me to one side and they both walked past me laughing. I was so filled with rage and so past caring.

'What did you call me?' I snarled.

'I called you a fucking twat, you fucking twat – you got a fucking problem with that, twat?'

Both angled up to me, fists tight, shoulders rolling, waiting for an excuse to hit me. I was happy to give it them. I pulled my arm back and landed one on Paul. I caught him hard against the left side of his nose. His blood started spilling and they were on me. They beat seven bells of shit out of me. I remember, as it was all going off, feeling strangely removed from it all. I wanted them to hurt me, to hit me and kick me and beat me and punish me, debase and humiliate me. And they did. Fists were flailing, raining down on me in every direction. Bashing the crap out of me. Punching and slapping and pounding into me. Boots giving me a shoeing, backwards and forwards with force, one after another, kicking and stamping and punting into me. My head was ringing and wet with blood. My clothes greedily sucking up all the piss on the floor. Bones aching and body bruised. It's a seminal moment in any man's life, the having the shit kicked out of him in a toilet episode. It hurt and didn't hurt. Hurts less than you think. The pain of it is irrelevant. It's the humiliation that counts. But I couldn't care. They punched me and kicked me and spat on me until they had had their fill – fully engorged and laughing.

As they left I could hear Johnny Cash on the juke box singing 'Folsom Prison Blues'. It made me smile and then I passed out.

When I came round I was lying in the street, slumped on my side next to a pile of bin bags. I'd been put out with the rubbish. Who put me out I don't know. People were walking past me, ambling home, to and fro. No-one seemed to pay me any mind. No-one even seemed to notice me. It made me feel so sad. So disappointed. And alone. I felt heartbroken...

I sat in the gutter, hiding my broken face in the rubbish, ashamed of myself and of my tears and of me. Ashamed of me, and my awful venal stinking self. Ashamed to be, or to have been. A rotten loathing, full of anger and revulsion, stewed within... The day had started so well, I thought of Milka, and cried... I cried... But no-one paid me any mind, no-one touched my shoulder, no-one even saw...

And on top of all of that, I've lost my compass.

# WEDNESDAY

I don't know what time I got in last night. The wind blew me home in a befuddled haze. A sad lump of loneliness stuck in my throat, feelings broken and choking, as I hacked my way up the Essex Road, walking all the way. Red lights swirling green into orange and blue, bleached and bleeding in the puddles and glass. Down the Balls Pond, one foot in front of the other, lamp lights fading, streets deserted, the slow plod backwards through the night till dawn, quiet and by myself. The unassuming inconspicuous halfway time between tomorrow and today, those slow frozen hours of in-between, they're something of a comfort to the drunk rolling home.

I got in and made myself a cup of the Earl, rolled a jazz cigarette strong enough to fell a woolly mammoth, and then lay on my bed in a sort of numb removed semi-conscious wired coma, twitching and tensing and grinding my teeth. The gouged-out ambushed ends of derangement. My face, my ribs and legs all aching and commiserating and complaining, trying to find some settled comfort. Eventually I managed to arrange myself in such a way as to not be in too much pain and passed out, but then had terrible troubled dreams. Strange tangled imaginings full of dark and twisted energy. Nightmares invading my subconscious, intruding and fiddling with me in the dead of night. It never ends, the long disgrace of life.

I dreamt of a man called Peter Crumb, but it wasn't Peter Crumb, it was someone else. He had blond hair and worked for Kent Social Services. He was standing in my bedroom watching me sleep. He was naked but for a green plastic name badge, pinned through a bloody scab on his left nipple. He approached me, leant over me and whispered something in my ear. I can't remember what. And then I woke and I was standing in the corridor. I could smell damp. It was familiar. He appeared and stared at me, and I at him, the same. He held out his hand and offered me two coins, gold coins. He dropped the coins into my hand and then, like a magician, smiled. I looked at the coins and saw that they were melting, thick dark chocolate was oozing out of them, sticky and gooey between my fingers. I looked at him and he shook his head. I looked back at the coins, and they were gone. My hands were covered in dark clods of blood. Valerie and Emma were lying on the floor. Something was wrong. They were wearing bikinis, whispering and giggling and making arrangements. I looked back at the man but his face had changed – it wasn't mine – he laughed and showed me a knife. A penknife, shaped like a fish, with a green and yellow handle. He handed Emma a bucket and spade, she took it from him smiling. The bucket was blue. He whispered something in her ear, I couldn't hear what, and then he slit her throat. There were newspapers laid out all over the floor. A wall-to-wall patchwork of obscene threatening headlines, and Emma and Valerie, dismembered. The sawn-off bits and pieces of them, laid out in no particular order – but arranged just so, placed and positioned, a head, a foot, an arm, a leg, a torso, a hand and so on… I was holding Emma's bucket – it was full of white sugar. I started scattering the sugar all over the floor. I knew that I had to do this, but I didn't know why.

'Remember that?' he suddenly barked. And I woke. My doorbell was ringing.

My face was encrusted with dry blood and stuck to the pillow. Scabs, bruises and bash marks, blue, yellow and purple, were punched into me and all over me. My left eye was heavily swollen, my lips split, bloody and tumid. Milka looked horrified. It was a fair reaction, I looked monstrous, literally like a monster. Poor girl. I didn't say anything, I didn't know what to say, I just opened the door and stared at her. She didn't say anything either, which I thought was telling, she didn't even ask if I was all right, she just took my arm and walked me slowly into the front room and sat me down. It was strange, and unusual, but I instinctively feel safe with Milka. She has no side, or seems not to, and is very young, but I digress. She went into the kitchen and came back with a bowl of warm water and a dry tea towel. She knelt down next to me and nursed my wounds, dipping the towel into the water and then padding me and wiping me. We didn't speak, I just let her get on with it. I closed my eyes and tried not to think. It was nice – the warm moistness, damping me. When she'd finished, she sat with me for a moment, noiseless and still, and looked troubled and concerned, as humans do. And then she said, 'Okay. I clean now.'

I nodded and shuffled back into the bedroom feeling weaned. It was a weird episode. Another weird episode.

She's been at it for two hours now. Scrubbing and washing and sweeping and hoovering, picking things up and putting stuff away, folding things and closing drawers – the washing machine is screaming. I spied on her cleaning the bathroom, she had her fingers down the plughole clearing out great tumorous glumps of knotted hair coated in a greasy soap and spat-back toothpaste gloop. It was vile. The rotting decomposing bits of me, lumping in a greasy pipe – urgh. A fitting end to you, Crumb – stuck in a blocked pipe. She's on her knees in the corridor at the moment, scrubbing the back of the front door, cleaning his dirty sperm stains. I'm hiding beneath my blankets, feeling ashamed, and writing this. A soggy bruised self-indulgent sadness warming me. He's hiding behind the coats in the wardrobe. He thinks I haven't seen him, but of course I have, the fool. He's always quiet after a night on the booze.

I think it's about eleven forty-five, but I'm not sure – I'm lost without my compass and I don't trust the inside clocks, they don't have arms, but it's Wednesday. There are five days standing. Two days down. And time rolls on.

I'm not going to go out today. It looks dirty, cold, uncomfortable and grey. A doleful, plaintive, London day… I'm going to hole up and stay in. Yes, it seems wise. I'm full of feelings – stuck-in-the-throat feelings that I can't make head nor tail of – gloomy, sullen feelings. The shameful effects of a paranoid hangover, I dare say, and the opium blues… Feelings… And memories.

There's a squirrel in the garden burying a scone…

Milka knocked on my door and said she was all done. I asked her what time it was. She said it was twelve fifteen. The short arm north, the long arm east. I gave her thirty pounds, she'd done a good job. Three hours' work, ten pound an hour – for a Pole she should be laughing. She said if I wanted she would go up the shops and get me some food – she said she saw the fridge was empty, and the cupboards. Her comments pricked me and made me feel ashamed and defensive. I told her not to worry about it. I said I'd go out later and get a kebab – which just sounded ridiculous. She insisted, saying I was 'injure'.

I couldn't be bothered to argue with her and was starving hungry so I said it was kind of her and gave her another twenty-pound note and made a small list of ingredients for a pot of brown. She left and took the key to let herself back in.

The flat is immaculate. It's amazing – the girl has done wonders, especially in the bathroom, I've never seen it so clean. Everything shining and polished. Towels folded, chrome glistening, soap on the side – pubes removed, a little flannel draped over the edge of the basin, my toothbrush with the toothpaste – cap on, in a glass – it was all like a Trust House Forte, an immaculate white brightness with the fervent stink of cleanliness tickling my nostrils. The pungent valour of health and hygiene, wholesome and unabashed. And the water in the toilet is blue. Bravo Milka! I felt awful sitting down to do my dump and dirtying the bowl. I thought perhaps I should do it in the kitchen bin to weigh down the new empty bin liner. But as things turned out I needn't have worried. This morning's stool was off the scale – it didn't appear, there wasn't one. An enormous crack of thundering wind and then nothing. Nothing but an awful sulphurous stink. I thought the Devil had entered.

The kitchen is a triumph too and a completely different colour. I've always thought of the kitchen as being a dark brown, but it turns out it's more of a light ochre. Everything is in its proper place and looking righteous and smelling proud. There's nothing on the floor, everything has been found a home or put away. All the furniture is arranged and placed and positioned. All the chairs in the front room are angled towards the television, and she's stacked all of the boxes in the spare room… I should get rid of those boxes, full of all that junk. Burn them all – make a bonfire in the garden and burn the bloody lot of it. All the captured bits of me, the scraps and pictures and notes and letters, burn it all, burn the lot of it – every last trace of me. Every last bit of me – up in flames and gone for good. Forgotten and gone. Rid me of these memories… Yes, that's something to do this afternoon. Get out into the garden, and burn the past… To ashes with it.

Milka returned with seven bags full of food and an assortment of extras from Tesco. Not a retailer I usually frequent, but I have to tell you, I couldn't believe it. I had no idea twenty pounds could buy so much. I normally just go to the Turks on the corner. I've suspected for some time that they have been overcharging me, and I confess I never check my change, so I've only myself to blame, but this is a revelation. I am almost forced to reconsider my socio-economic standing. Now all of a sudden I'm a Tesco Finest man. Organic, no less!

Milka is non-stop. She's like a force of nature. A bright white chimera, vivid with electric blonde locks crackling wild with static. She put everything away. Opening and closing cupboards and drawers. Stacking boxes and tins and emptying and clearing and throwing away. In and out of the fridge. Chopping and peeling and sparking up the old Baby Belling. She knows her way around the kitchen better than I do. She has the natural way of a woman about her – knowing where everything is, moving from this to that – it's like watching a dance, and because my eye is so swollen it appeared at times as if there were two of her, performing a sort of ghost-like synchronized kitchen pas de deux. It was beautiful. Not like me and him lumbering about and bashing into everything. In next to no time she'd rustled up a pot of thick broth, steaming hot and bubbling away, scents and smells seeping into everywhere. You could smell it all over the house. She even set the table. Something I haven't seen since… Hmm. A place mat. One spoon, one napkin. A side plate and a challah. It all looked so lonely.

'Please,' I said, 'won't you join me?'

'No, I okay,' she said. 'I just stand. Is okay – you eat – is okay. I stand.'

And so we had lunch together, me sat by myself at the table, she standing, leaning against the fridge.

Her broth was delicious. And just what I needed. It filled me and restored me, warmed me through and left me glowing. She's a lovely all right. A beautiful hallucination in blue velour sweatpants – her pert little bottom sticking out behind. Fragile and delicate and porcelain white and kind. Her lips are a perfect pink. And she's a quiet one too. Hardly says anything at all. She just gets on with it. You feel safe with her, at ease with her. It's strange for me to feel this, but I think I trust her. I said to her, 'Thank you for all you've done this morning, Milka. You've been very kind.' She cleared my bowl and said, 'Is okay. You injure.'

She put the dishes in the sink and started running the taps. I sat silently watching her. Her body slumped forward over the sink, one shoulder higher than the other, the slow gentle tumble of pots splashing and knocking. The radiators pumping, thickening the air… It made everything slow. And then I don't know why but all of a sudden I felt very awkward and uncomfortable. I started to imagine things that she might be thinking, bad things about me, and so I got up and traipsed back into the bedroom. I don't know why I started thinking, and I don't know why I got up and left her, I just did – just to move, I suppose, and dissipate the oddness. I do feel odd when I'm with humans, even if they're lovelies like Milka – I get to feeling difficult and stiff, especially if there's a silence. I just start moving, sometimes it's just my head that moves, looking up or sideways, other times it's my legs jiggling or crossing and uncrossing, or it's my arms folding and unfolding or scratch-ing, often it's scratching, and then sometimes it's all of me, moving randomly from one place to another without any moti-vation or reason, or consideration for the situation – which is what I did in this instance. Milka was washing the pots, I sud-denly felt odd, and then stood up and traipsed to the bedroom, feeling glum for doing so and hoping she wouldn't think me weird but suspecting that she already does. I don't understand myself and am forced to conclude that having insight into one's own condition is no guarantee of control over it. It's a bummer. Anyway, when I got to the bedroom he was watching me, but said nothing, just stared at me from behind the coats in the wardrobe. I knew what he was thinking – and it was hate-ful. I ignored him and looked at myself in the mirror – a horri-fying deformed monster. It made me feel sad, sad like Quasimodo. I shuffled back into the kitchen and found Milka drying the last of the washing up.

'I was wondering,' I said, scratching my head and then fold-ing and unfolding my arms. 'Those boxes in the spare room. I've been meaning to get rid of all that junk for ages now. I was wondering – if you're not doing anything this afternoon – I was wondering if you could help me burn it all in the garden?'

She said she'd be happy to. It was as simple as that.

We carried all the boxes out the back and stacked them in the garden in three uneven piles, awkwardly leaning and about to topple. I went round the front and got one of the old galvanized rubbish bins, emptied all the crap in it out onto the pavement and then dragged it round the back. One of the towers had collapsed, a couple of boxes had split and burst and spilt their contents all over the grass. Milka was on her hands and knees gathering it all back together.

'Chuck it all in here,' I said, setting the bin down.

She picked up the split boxes and emptied their contents into the bin. Photographs, letters, diaries, tumbled, torn and twisted. I emptied a half-litre of white spirit over it all, lit a match and threw it in. The bin exploded, bursting into flames, a greedy inferno, ravenously licking the air. We watched it for a moment and then slowly began to feed the rest of my past into it. I could see her looking at the photographs of me and Valerie and Emma. I could see her noiselessly having thoughts – but she didn't say anything. She didn't need to ask, or have it explained. She knew, and stayed silent, diligently feeding the recorded moments of my life into the fire. Burning me. She understood. It revealed a cold, detached hardness in her that I liked. She caught me watching her and smiled at me, and then dropped thirty-four frozen Kodak moments of a holiday in Cyprus onto the passionately flaming entries in a half-burnt diary I kept as a teenager. I'd have liked to have re-read that diary. Steamy stuff, as I recall – all bullshit, of course, teenage dribblings – but still, it would have whiled away an hour.

'Burn it – burn it all,' I kept repeating. The boxed forgotten proof of my existence. The personal unremembered bits and pieces of us all, the letters and keepsakes, the mementos, remnants, heirlooms, tokens and trophies. The useless minutiae of nothing very much at all, kept solely to remind… Photographs, hundreds and hundreds of photographs – the tyranny of photography, every moment of my life captured and paraded – from nappies through shorts into trousers. Sleeping infancy and my first steps, my first teeth, my first birthday, my first Christmas, my first day at school – marked, appraised and boxes ticked. My first car – Toyota Corolla, yellow – stolen in Leeds, found burnt in Manchester. My first girlfriend – Lisa Jackson. My first flat – another squalid shithole. A Cub Scout in uniform toggled up tight. A boy in corduroys with strange hair and a jumper. Skid-mark expressions, tedious posturing, affected displays of normality. Rough approximations of something like the others and time's unsparing way with it all. A mother and a father at this age and that, in this house and that. On holiday here, on holiday there. Christmas, Easter, summer in the sunshine, the winter it snowed. A boy called David Warner – remember him? I camped in his back garden aged eleven. It was an awful night. I had a terrible cold and couldn't stop sneezing. I desperately wanted to blow my nose but didn't have a handkerchief and so kept on sniffing. I knew my sniffing was keeping David awake. And I knew it was annoying him, but he didn't say anything, he just kept huffing and sighing and tutting, miffed. I wanted him to like me.

I remember feeling so embarrassed. Frightened in a tent, aged eleven, sniffing and sorrying from dusk till dawn. In the end I blew my nose into my underpants. Just one of the many calamitous childhood atrocities I was made to endure on the road to manhood and eventual madness.

I remember that night for other reasons too. It was the night that David's dad left him. He woke the following morning to find that his father had gone. Just upped and gone in the dead of night, never to be seen again. It affected David, and I felt sorry for him. Run off with another woman, said Dad. Men are all bastards, said Mum. Burn, say I. And burn. Burn the bloody lot – be rid of me. That brazen, peevish juvenile – skulking and parading, the fraud. The liar. Impostor. Pretender. I was there, I saw it! I did it! And look at me, look at me, look at me! The legion of me. The innumerable manys of me, me, me. Every moment and episode. The christening, the wedding, the funeral, the wake, the receptions and sunsets and more bloody sunsets – endless bloody sunsets – and views and culture and tears and beaches. I went there, I saw that, I did this, I've done that, I knew him, I had her, that was me, that was mine, this was there and that was that. Every step taken from the cradle to the grave brought to you bright from Happy Snaps. Quality control applies. The amazing magnificent glorious red-eyed moments of my life. To hell with them all and burn! Burn the bloody lot. Burn it.

'Chuck the whole bloody lot on,' I grumbled, troubled, thrashing around wildly for another box – grabbing one and tipping its entire contents in at once and then throwing the box in after – arms trembling, Milka watching. All those little moments, tumbling urgently into the flames, all those memories curling and blistering and raging – green and blue and orange, licking and peeling, chewing me into flaming oblivion… Be rid of me… Be rid of me.

There was a letter from Valerie. It was in my hand. Her last letter. The one with the line 'Nao he nada, senao que matao a meu marido.' I handed it to Milka. She read it, pausing at the Portuguese, and then looked at me for explanation. I translated: 'It is nothing, they are only killing my husband.' She smiled and then dropped the letter into the fire. It floated for a moment, held suspended in the heat above the flames, and then delicately danced ablaze. We watched it burn.

Milka handed me an old school report. The headmaster's comments were: 'A good term – did well in the field project, but could ask more questions. Good to see Peter settling down, although Mr Gretner has had cause to mention expressions of temperament twice this term – but I am pleased to say that the worst of last year seems to be behind us. Let us hope Peter can maintain this. Excellent performance as Bumble in the school play.'

Milka smiled. I don't know why, but her smile means so much to me. It touches me. And moves me… Is that my conscience? Or my feelings?

She opened another box. It was full of the newspapers with reports of Emma's death. She stopped before tipping them into the flames and looked at me, it was as if she knew.

I couldn't bear it. I was still in my pyjamas and dressing gown. I went indoors, leaving Milka to finish the job. I watched her from the bedroom window, flickering ghost-like through the flames, leafing through the last of me, and burning me.

'Been through you with a fine-tooth now,' he said, stepping out of the wardrobe and helping me into my overcoat. 'She knows it all now. She knows all about it. Seen all around and been into every inch of you hasn't she?'

He was right.

'She saw Emma's picture in the paper – she read the reports, she knows what happened – she knows who you are – she's seen into you, seen through you.'

He was right. The light bulb in the hallway flickered. Through the window I could see her opening the last of the boxes. All of Emma's clothes. Her little jumpers and little dresses, her little shoes and little socks. All the little bits, and all the little bobs, of a little life lost... The flames licked high, crackling bright... All was gone.

She stood watching the last of it burn. I thought how like an angel she appeared – abstract and ultra real. A vivid white imagining.

'She's the angel of death,' he said.

'I know,' I said, and looked away ashamed.


Milka left at four fifteen... I told her I'd see her next Wednesday and gave her the spare set of keys. I said if I'm out just let yourself in, I'll leave your money in an envelope on the side. She smiled and said okay.

She'll be the one that finds me. She'll be the one that tells my tale. She'll say kind things, and remember gentle truths.


The flat seemed so empty after she'd gone. I shuffled from room to room listening to the silence and the hollow nothingness of no-one else. I stood in the spare room for quite a long time staring at a stain on the carpet that looks like a screaming face. Every carpet's got one. Then I got back into bed and wrote everything down and started remembering it all over again. Replaying it all in an endless loop. Round and round it goes. There's never any forgetting. The twisted cycle of remembrance, unendurable pain and intolerable embarrassment. He said I should go to sleep and dream it off. He was kind to me and tucked his hands gently under my chin, being careful of my bruises. All of it was coming back to me. All the horrid details. And the burning.

When I woke it was dark. I felt confused and out of sorts. I was tangled in the blankets and still wearing my overcoat and sweating profusely. I sat up and was suddenly aware of someone sitting in the shadows watching me. I turned sharply with a start to see who it was. At first I thought it was him. But it wasn't. The figure stood and moved slowly towards me. It was Milka. She was dressed in Emma's burnt and singed christening gown. Her eyes a pixellated red. She whispered something that I didn't understand, and then I woke... The house was silent. I sat on the edge of my bed. I felt so confused and abstracted. All these terrible dreams. Bloody opium. Everything out of kilter – time, and what to do.

I found a copy of today's *Metro* that Milka must have left behind. No mention of Monday's antics, the Sudder Street scandal. I'm half tempted to return to the scene of the crime, and see if anyone's found them yet, but won't – the spineless morality of the consequentialist in me prevents. The headline today by the way read:

# TOMMY COOPER FOUND IN FISHCAKE

Hmm?… I pondered whilst making a pot of brown.

**Peter Crumb's Pot of Brown**

Ingredients:

*One large onion*
*Two handfuls of small button mushrooms*
*Two cloves of garlic*
*Two bay leaves*
*Two cubes of Oxo*
*One small tin of double concentrate tomato purée*
*One tin of kidney beans (optional)*
*Two tins of chopped tomatoes*
*Four lumps of dark chocolate*
*Two fat handfuls of lean minced beef*

Finely chop the onion and brown till golden in a hot pan. Chop and add the mushrooms and stir on a medium to strong heat for five minutes. In a separate pan brown the mince and then add the onions and mushrooms. Chop and add the garlic, bay leaves, Oxo, tomato purée, tinned tomatoes, kidney beans and chocolate. Season, stir, and then leave on a low heat for about an hour. Serve hot with rice or a challah.

*Serves one person all week.*

... It was the incongruity of it that made me think of the squirrel. The story itself was perfectly straightforward. It involved a pensioner choking to death on a small plastic keyring of Tommy Cooper that had somehow found its way into a fishcake. Nothing odd about that, I agree. But it made me think of the squirrel and its scone. I couldn't stop thinking about it. So I went out into the garden to find the little devil's booty and dig it up. It didn't take long. I went to the spot where I'd seen him digging, saw the up-turned earth, got down on my hands and knees and dug until I found it. It was still whole but very soggy and infested with soil. As I was digging I noticed that the nosy curtain-twitching bugger that lives upstairs was watching me. I knew what I was doing was strange and I knew I looked odd, on my knees in the garden in my overcoat and pyjamas digging up an old scone, but I thought how dare he? How dare he watch me? I've always been a head-turner, I concede, but this I thought was too much – it's an intrusion! Brazenly eyeing me, in my own back garden – how dare he? Don't be intimidated, Crumb, I told myself – what you do in your own back garden is your business and nobody else's. I felt like a feminist with my tits out on a sunny afternoon. Let him watch, I thought. Watch all you bloody want, you pillock. You pervert. You gutless coward.

I dusted the scone, smelt it and put it in my pocket. Then I found a stick, crossed to the blackened burnt-out dustbin and gave the smouldering charred remains a poke and a stir. The ash was so fine and powdered, everything had burnt, all had gone, mingled into one, ashes to ashes, and starting to rain... I glanced at the sky, the first few heavy drops of a downpour were slowly starting to fall, and the goon upstairs was still watching me – there he was, a shadow in the window, twitching behind his curtains, the timorous dolt. I discarded the stick and leant forward over the dustbin and then reached down into its dark interior and plunged my hands into the still warm ash. It was so soft – like flour. I played with it, tumbling it between my palms, turning it over and rubbing it into my skin. It was nice, and so warm. I don't know why but for some reason it made me smile. Right, I thought, let's really give him something to remember – let's really give him something to gossip about with the others at those meetings they all have to discuss the carpet in the corridor. Yes, those meetings they never invite me to. Those meetings they think I don't know they have. Residents? What the fuck am I? Yes this'll give him something to complain about – keep him feeling connected and superior – the turd. Yes, come on, Crumb – I was starting to giggle – come on, Crumb – give him a real proper madman show, give him real proper bonkers. I pulled off my overcoat and unbuttoned my pyjama top, stripping myself naked to the waist. Why stop there? I heard myself consider. My fingers pulled my drawstrings and my pyjama bottoms dropped around my ankles, exposing my fleshy distended manhood. There was something elemental in it – certainly something mental in it – something African and wild, a crackpot connection with nature, sensual and hungry as the rain wet my body. The middle classes travel halfway around the world to see this sort of thing, I thought – and my penis was semi-erect, which both surprised and delighted me. I ceremonially lifted the dustbin high above my head and then tipped its contents out all over me. A hot black cloud of ash billowed all about me, shimmering in the moon-light, its particles glistening in the cold wet air, coating me in a fine grey patina. It was beautiful. I could taste it. My hands were working it into my face and around my neck, over my body, and between my legs and through my hair, encasing me in a thick crust of ash – burning me and stinging my cuts. That'll show him, I thought. That'll show him.

I came back inside and looked at myself in the mirror. I had to laugh. The folly that lives beneath – swollen, naked and painted grey. What a monster. I cackled like a loon, very loudly – Hahahaha! Hahahaha! Hahaahah! I could hear him anxiously pacing about upstairs, wondering what was to follow. I put the scone on a dainty side plate, dressed it up nicely with a pat of rancid butter and a dollop of apricot preserve (damp goes with butter and mud is not unlike apricot in texture), threw on my overcoat and went upstairs. I'm taking it up to him, I said, and I'm finally going to have it out with him. This has been going on for years and frankly it's intolerable. I've been meaning to have a word since the day I moved in. Skittish feelings of inferi-ority have so far prevented, but not any more, I'm knocking on his door and saying hello.

I shouldn't have, it was a terrible mistake… What bloody evil followed remains now and forever.

I stormed up the stairs to confront him. A jittery consciousness pushing at the awkward edges of unease, a knotted goading invasion of nausea and dread and an acid spike of hatred kin-dling within. I smudged butter and ash over his spyhole – I didn't want to ruin the surprise, rang his doorbell and waited, ears pricked, listening. I could hear him gutlessly crawling around under his bed, summoning the courage to answer – the pathetic cunt. After about five minutes and five more doorbell rings of various lengths, I at last heard his frightened cautious shuffle down the corridor towards me, and then a timorous enquiring: 'Yes?'

'Hello,' I said, loudly and with confidence. 'It's your neighbour. Could you open up?'

There was a brief pause, and then he bashfully piped, 'What do you want?'

'I thought I'd come and introduce myself,' I said, sounding as reasonable and as mild-mannered and as sane as I could. There was another pause.

'I see,' he said, rather knowingly. It momentarily confused me, and I remember noting a tick in my thinking. With hindsight I realize I should have paid that tick a lot more mind.

'It's a little inconvenient at the moment,' he went on, stammering excuses and bluffing polite go-aways. 'I was about to turn in, couldn't it wait until the morning?'

The cunning swine – of course it could wait, all things can wait – got to get on with them, though, haven't we? – vexing me with his possibilities and alternatives and damnable choices. Turn in to what I wondered? Think of something, Crumb. My mind was racing and then I remembered the scone.

'I've brought you something,' I gleefully continued. 'A peace offering. I just wanted to say hello and introduce myself. I should have popped round years ago I know but… well, better late then never…'

There was another pause – slightly longer this time. Come

on, I thought, open up… My luck was in, his about to run out. I heard the key turn in the lock. The fool, I thought – he's let his manners get the better of him, he's told himself that he's being ridiculous and that his suspicions about his neighbour are nothing to worry about and that everything will be all right and that human beings are essentially good. I don't need to put the safety chain on, he's thought – that'll seem hostile and suspicious and untrusting, be friendly he's told himself, you've nothing to be afraid of, be confident and smile. The fool – he had everything to fear. He turned the key and opened his door. If only he hadn't. Never open your door to strangers at night, however rude it may feel.

'Hello,' I said, as gracious as a vicar on a Sunday afternoon, expansively offering him my hand and stepping forward into his space. 'My name's Peter. It's joyful to meet you – I've brought you a scone.'

You should have seen his expression. He didn't know what to think or where to look or what to say. He was quaking. There I was, my features swollen, blackened with ash, smiling like a minstrel and offering a scone – he nearly shat his pants.

'I just thought I'd pop round and introduce myself,' I said again. 'We've been neighbours for years now. I've often seen you about, coming and going, twitching behind the curtains, pacing up and down – I thought I'd bring you an offering and say hello.' I pushed the plate and scone forward into his hands, forcing him to take it. The poor man was terrified. He just stood there staring at me, so I smiled at him – a real big toothy beamer, which seemed to scare him even more. His muscles twitched, involuntarily pulling him backwards. He was like a frightened child, cowering. This was too easy. It was pathetic. I could hear his kettle reaching the boil and the switch clicking loud. He's got a metal kettle, I thought. One of those posh ones. Plastic kettles click quiet.

'Have you got a brew on?' I enthused, pointing down his corridor and stepping past him. 'Which way is it – through here?'

'Please – I'm sorry – No – Please –' he hurriedly babbled behind me. I ignored him. The layout of his flat was exactly as mine, I turned right and stepped into his living room.

'Well well well – who's this then?'

Sitting straight-backed, bolt upright on the sofa was a dark-haired bespectacled woman staring at me. Her mouth was open and her hands held out in front of her, frightened palms facing, and ever so slightly shaking. She didn't say anything, she was too scared to.

'Hello,' I said. 'My name's Peter. I live beneath. I just thought I'd pop up and introduce myself. I've brought you a scone. Only the one, I'm afraid. To be honest I didn't realize there were two of you.'

They were both staring at each other. This was their nightmare come true. A blacked-up semi-naked madman in their living room. They'd read about this in the papers. Every evil imagining was flitting through their frightened minds. I didn't really want to scare them – certainly not terrify them. I was just having some fun. Taking advantage of their smug middle-class window-locked concerns and their ABC1 fear and paranoia – playing with them, teasing them, that's all. But they weren't amused. It was obvious they thought I was care in the community gone wrong, gone horribly wrong. They honestly thought that I was going to do something awful to them, gut them or something. She had rape on her mind, I could tell. It saddened me to think that that's how I'm perceived. People look at me, I'm aware of that, I've grown accustomed to the stranger's eye being on me, as I've said – I've always been a head-turner. But you are what others make of you, Crumb – and what these two made of me was obvious, an unhinged corruption of the human condition let loose in their front room with evil intent. A criminally insane painted monster. It's too black and white to be true but what do you expect, Crumb? You turn up in the middle of the night all but naked, covered in ash, offering scones, and you think folks aren't going to wonder?... You're right, I've only myself to blame – but still, I digress...

'D'you mind if I sit down?' I said, and not waiting for a reply I parked my arse in a big white armchair and settled comfortably back, sighing like an aunt at a funeral.

The bespectacled woman looked at me, closed her gob, swallowed and then said, 'Please... We were about to go to bed...' A tight, mean little accent grovelled in the back of her throat.

'You're German,' I immediately blurted.

'Yes,' she said, and we paused and took stock.

'Well I never,' I said. 'I know a German – he's called Dieter. He sells drugs. Do you know him?'

They looked at each other and then back at me. Their disturbed expressions jellied into clotted consternation. There was another pause. It made me nervous and suddenly I felt I had to say something, so I said the only thing I know how to say in German: 'Arbeit macht frei!' And then raised my eyebrows and smiled. It was idiotic, and insensitive. I felt foolish and looked away.

The television was flickering in the corner – an Asian homo-sexual was solemnly regurgitating the day's events… I thought for a moment and then remembered that there's an order in which things are done, and that asking people their names is one of the first things to do when getting to know.

'What are your names?' I politely enquired. They again looked at each other. And then back at me.

'My name's Beth, and this is Adrian.' She sounded embar-rassed. Her voice was wavering. He said nothing. The wimp. It was obvious who wore the trousers in this relationship. There was another pause – unbearably long, yawning between us. Not a lively pair of conversationalists, these two, I thought – no, they're the sort that suck, that's what they are – drains, not ra-diators. It made me angry and I felt my blood thickening. Everything was awkward and tangibly at odds. It's funny what uncomfortable creatures human beings are, how sticky and anile we feel with each other.

'I see you've got the floorboard effect,' I randomly contin-ued, clutching at conversational straws, crossing my legs and noticing my toenails. They're a fearsome sight, I haven't cut them in ages. Dirty cracked yellow talons curling beneath me. I felt dirty and neglected like an Archway schnorrer.

'It's a popular look these days, isn't it?' I went on. 'The floor effect… That'll be why I'm always hearing you pacing… Yes, and bashing about, dropping things… Fucking great clattering noises you two make, don't you? Scares the fucking wits out of me sometimes. All of a sudden a great fucking smashing noise and then the pacing up and down and it all echoes with a floor like that, doesn't it?... It's like a bloody echo chamber in here, isn't it?... And I can hear you piss!' I chuckled, pointing at Adrian and winking at Beth. 'He goes like a bloody horse, doesn't he?'

She wasn't amused.

'I prefer a carpet myself,' I went on. 'But there you are, it takes all sorts...'

I couldn't think of anything else to say after that and so stopped, uncrossed my legs, leant forward, tucked my palms beneath my knees and stared at my cock through a fold in my overcoat. I used to sit like this when I was a little boy, I thought, and I remembered myself aged ten. I suddenly felt very weak and yielding... What am I doing? I thought. Why on earth had I intruded on these people? The edges of my mouth peeled south. Here they were quietly enjoying their evening, watching the news, about to go to bed and perhaps have a bunk-up, and then I barge in, scaring them and disgracing myself. I felt a heated pang of intense conscience hit me. It surged from deep inside me and scoured through me. There it is, I thought – you see, you do have a conscience, you're a good man, Crumb. And then for a moment, a very brief moment, I felt happy. Happy in a sad way. Conscious of myself in an innocent way, guileless and free, ten years old and unafraid. Yes, I thought, you're all right, Crumb – you're a good man at heart... And then my testicles heaved, my scrotum contracted, my skin horripilated and a mad rash of goose pimples ran villainously over my thighs and up my spine, tingling me with a devilish cold. I felt ridiculous and emotional, and started scratching myself and crossing and uncrossing my ankles. I felt exposed and guilty. I pulled my coat close around me, and thought of him downstairs, the canker, hiding in the wardrobe and blushed.

Beth, being a woman, immediately sensed this change in me and then, being a woman, immediately went on the offensive. Wielding gentleness and calm she softly said, 'Well, it's nice to have met you, Peter… But it's late now and we were just about to go to bed… So if you don't mind… Perhaps we'll see you again soon.' And then she smiled. But it wasn't like Milka's smile. There was something wrong with it. Something not quite right about it. And she knew it. I held her gaze, remained seated, and said nothing. The atmosphere soured. I took a deep breath, sighed with obvious disappointment and then started wriggling my toes on the plastic floorboards, making a scratching noise with my toenails that sounded like insects scuttling. They were watching me, intently – uncertain of how to proceed, how to get rid of me. Adrian was still holding the plate with the scone. He looked like such a twat.

'You are going to eat that scone, aren't you?' I enquired with a nonchalant but caustic aggression.

'Yes, of course,' he nervously replied, smiling falsely.

'Go on then.'

'Well, I don't know that I'm going to eat it this instant. I thought I might perhaps have it a little later.'

'You said you were about to go to bed.'

'Well yes, I mean – I thought I might have it in the morning and then pop the plate round.'

I paused in the clichéd dramatic fashion and then said, very deliberately said: 'I think you should eat it now.'

He looked at me and sort of laughed as though I were joking. I remained silent, deadly serious, staring at him. 'Eat it now,' I demanded, raising my voice. He looked alarmed. 'I'm sorry to be so suspicious but you know what people are like. You can't trust anybody these days,' I indignantly asserted, raising my eyebrows. 'For all I know, the moment I've gone, you're going to throw it in the bin. So if you don't mind – I think it's the least you can do, after all the trouble I've been to digging it up. If you don't mind – I don't think I'm being unreasonable – I'd like to see you eat it.' I stopped and waited to see what the gutless little bed-wetter would do.

'I don't really feel like it at the moment,' he replied, trying to assert himself.

'Well, perhaps Beth wants it,' I said, upping the ante.

'Look,' he said with a certain swagger, intervening, determined not to make a complete coward of himself. 'I'm sorry to have to say this, but could you please just leave.'

I gave him the long pause, and the look that goes with it. I could hear them both breathing – it was funny, their breathing was backward, like mine in the morning. I saw his right hand tremble and the scone wobble. Beth was more together. She calmly lifted her palm and said, placating, 'We're very tired, Peter.' Cunning use of my name, I thought, making it personal – I bet she's been on a course and had training. 'We've had a long hard day, it's very nice to meet you, and thank you for the scone, but we'd like to go to bed now, Peter.'

'I'm sorry, Beth, but in England we simply don't behave in this way. I'm not going until I've seen you eat that scone. And then I'll take my plate and go.'

'Oh for God's sake!' Adrian suddenly burst out, pushing the plate and scone back towards me. 'Take your bloody plate and go!'

I looked at him and started laughing in a very demeaning, sneering and spiteful way, which really seemed to ignite him.

'Look,' he said huffing and puffing, 'if you don't go I'm going to have to call the police.'

'And what are they going to do, Adrian? Arrest me for being neighbourly?'

'Look, we've tried to be polite. I'm asking you one last time – please will you leave.'

'Not until you've eaten that scone.'

'Take your plate and go.'

'It's not about the fucking plate!' I barked, angrily jumping to my feet and wildly swinging my arm, violently cracking Adrian across his face, knocking the plate out of his hands and sending the scone flying across the room. It hit the wall, stuck for a moment, and then fell to the floor. The plate smashed, shattering to pieces, and clattering everywhere with great effect.

'All right, all right,' Adrian protested – panicking, his voice faltering with tearful mobility. 'Please – calm down, everything's all right. I'll eat the bloody scone.' And then they both fell to their knees and hurriedly picked the damp soggy soiled lumps of crumbling scone up off the floor and tossed them into their frightened mouths.

There was a pause… Quite a long pause… All three of us were wondering what was going to happen next. I stood over them, staring down at them, cowering at my feet. They were utterly terrified – their faces were twitching and blinking. Adrian's leg was shaking uncontrollably like a frightened dog. It was truly pathetic. They had sublimated their will entirely to mine. And all it took was one cuff across his chops. What cosseted lives they must have led. Beth was making whimpering noises and crying, shaking and moaning. Her tears, her fear, her confusion, her helplessness were all undoing her, drawing her backwards into herself, a terrified foetal hysteria gestating into desperation. She wanted Adrian – 'her man' – to do something. But she knew he wouldn't, she knew there was nothing within his impotent resources that he could do. I stared at them and felt my face break into that slow malevolent sneer. I know I was being a bully, but the fuckers deserved it. He was such a little twerp. He was so wet and pathetic and weak. He could have said no – he could have protested, stood up for himself and fought me – he could have risked something – the spineless, gutless coward. It's not like I was bigger than him, if anything he was bigger than me. It enraged me – such yellow timidity. What kind of a sex life must these two have – I bet she's always on top, it's the fashion these days.

I was about to turn and leave when I noticed that Adrian's attention had been drawn towards the television. I turned and looked. At first I was confused – I didn't quite understand what I was seeing, or rather I couldn't quite believe what I was seeing. For there in front of me on their television screen was a scratchy tinted picture taken from a CCTV camera of me. Quite unmistakably me. That handsome but melancholy devil that I wake up to every day was there before me – live on regional television. The Sudder Street scandal in all its lurid gruesome glory was being broadcast to the region – and there I was, 'wanted' for questioning by a troubled-looking Detective Inspector John Marsden. He used the words 'ferocious' and 'vicious' and 'wild' and 'savage'. He might have used the word 'evil', I thought, but he didn't, they're so secular, the police. He said someone must know this man, and warned, 'If you see him do not approach him.' Well well well, I thought – I'm a celebrity!

I calmly picked up the remote control and turned the television off. Beth and Adrian were now silent and staring at me – their eyes wide, Beth's mouth again open. In spite of the ash and bruises they knew it was me, there was no mistaking it. I turned and walked quickly out of the sitting room, down the corridor and into their kitchen. I knew what I had to do. I had to kill them both. Not to do so was not an option, there was no doubt in my mind – it was a matter of conscience. I had to do it. I pulled a large murderous-looking carving knife from the magnetic strip next to the oven and returned to the sitting room.

Adrian was reaching for the telephone, his fingers panicking, fumbling, trying to dial, but he didn't have enough time. I swung my arm fast and stabbed him in the side of his neck. The blade entered his throat behind his Adam's apple, passed swiftly through his neck and then emerged, bloodily, out the other side. I twisted the blade and then sliced the knife forward, out through the front of his throat, severing his neck in two. A torrent of blood spurted in all directions, cascading down the front of him and all over me. He fell to his knees and then slumped forward into the large white armchair. I turned to face Beth. She was standing stock still, frozen, with her hands to her mouth. Without hesitation I stabbed her in the stomach. It was strange. Stabbing someone is not as easy as you may think. The blade entered her belly and then, after about two inches' penetration, stopped. Her stomach muscles were gripping the blade. I had to really force the remaining six inches into her, and turning the blade inside her, to make sure the wound was fatal, proved almost impossible – and pulling the blade back out of her required maximum strength and both hands. But I got it done. She fell to the floor and rolled onto her back, holding her belly and bleeding profusely. It was shocking to see just how much blood there was. In the moments that it took to dispatch them – and it was only moments – a massive amount of blood had been spilt, and neither of them were yet dead. Adrian was holding his throat, opening and closing his mouth, coughing up great mouthfuls of blood. Beth lay perfectly still, pressing her palms against her wound, hopelessly trying to staunch the flow. Thankfully neither of them was making too much noise, so I sat down on the sofa and waited for them both to die. It was at this point that I noticed I had an enormous erection – but I paid it no mind.

Adrian died quite quickly, overacting all the way. His jugular had been cut and he was losing massive amounts of blood. It took only minutes, but he played every moment to the hilt – coughing and spluttering and... honestly, I thought, he's going for the fucking Oscar! But then, quite comically, he just stopped and was dead, and that was that. Beth on the other hand gave a much more understated performance. She simply lay there holding her stomach, taking slow shallow breaths. She must have been in extraordinary pain but you wouldn't have known it to look at her. She looked like she had a bit of a headache or a mild period pain, nothing more serious than that. She didn't cry, she didn't call out, she didn't even moan – Germans, I thought, there's restraint for you. She would occasionally close her eyes and then open them again – a sort of extended blinking – but other than that, nothing – no histrionics, no carry-on at all. Bravo, I thought. Good for you, Beth. Dignified even in death. She rolled her head to face me, her spectacles fell and she put her eyes on me – her pretty hazel eyes, watching me... And then it struck me – she was really quite attractive. I hadn't noticed before, but looking at her now, laid out on the floor before me – so quiet and still – she was really very attractive. Not beautiful, but handsome. Her features were strong, carved with a wanton brooding intensity. Her hair was dark and scattered wildly about her. She was wearing a simple green springtime dress – a halter neck, I think they call it. The ones without a back where the front ties behind the neck, the kind of dress you can't wear a bra with, the kind of dress you can peel a girl out of with ease. Her skin was a faded olive grey, her lips a matching blue, full and round and endlessly kissable. Her thighs were fuller than the fashion of today allows and her legs proportionally shorter than her body, but her bosom was ample and her lines curvaceous. Yes, I thought – you're really very handsome, aren't you, Beth? Comely, womanly and sensual. Yes, I thought – a sensualist. Her feet were bare and only inches from mine, and such pretty little feet they were too – cute, pudgy little feet with tiny toes and painted nails, a bright slut red, very racy. I extended my foot towards hers and gently started to tickle the wrinkled folded undersides of her arches with my toenails – scratching and teasing. Her toes twitched and then twitched again, she was still alive. Our eyes met – her pretty hazel eyes and mine, held, as the morbid pull of sex and death prickled between us and a perverted hankering stirred in my loins. My erection remembered and its purple end throbbed... I got up, grabbed her by the ankles and dragged her down the corridor towards the bedroom. Polished imitation laminate wood flooring is ideal for dragging bodies hither and thither.

# THURSDAY

We woke with our ankles tangled, spooning. The forbidding intimacy of skin on skin, her nakedness and ruin cold in my arms, and the sour stink of blood and death and murder pungent in the stale air. A nightmare of thoughts and feelings was seething in my soul. What had I done?

He was standing in the corner of the room, watching me, his rotten allies – memory, conscience and evil – crowding in behind. I waited for him to speak, to drool his mean good morning, but he didn't, he just stared at me and said nothing. It was strange, but I didn't panic, quite the reverse, I felt a profound calm – an obliging, relaxed quiescence, easy in my bones. Ahh – I thought – the effects of an expensive mattress, and duck-down pillows. Normally I wake in excruciating pain, but not today, today I am calm and relaxed. I know this will sound odd, but I felt like a pregnant woman. That is to say, I felt superior in my human qualities.

I got up and wandered through into the sitting room, following the blood trail and taking in the sights. A veritable bloodbath of butchery, carnage and slaughter. I've never seen so much blood and viscera – ripped, torn, gutted, splattered and smeared. All over the walls, all over the floor, all over the furniture, and all over me. Blood upon blood upon blood. A scene of brutal cruelty, of unimaginable suffering. Abominable, wicked and evil, and the slow dawning realization that it was all mine... I did this. I did it. I slit his throat. I gutted his wife. I took her and used her. I put my evil into her, as she lay dying... I did this.

But as I said, I didn't panic. I calmly ran a bath and had a good soak, availed myself of Beth and Adrian's extensive range of lotions, oils and unguents, scrubbed myself clean, shaved, washed my hair and cut my toenails... I got out of the bath a new man – a coconut-and-apple-scented man, exfoliated, cleansed and conditioned. I sat on the edge of the bath and stared at myself in the mirror. There was something different, something had changed, there was an otherness about me that puzzled and held me in vain regard for some time. My peeled-clean nakedness an admirable delight to behold... And the scab on my ankle is healing.

He seemed different too. He was sitting on the toilet, musing... He seemed sombre, and still hadn't spoken, which, as I've said, I did think was strange. He's a chatterer by nature, not the taciturn type at all. Neurotic in his need to be thinking, and even more so in his urge for it all to be out loud. But not this morning. It was as if he was trying to remember something but couldn't, and was stuck on the same thought – locked in a moment's recollection that he couldn't escape. He also seemed to fear me, and know, instinctively, that I was not the sort of man that one should anger. It pleased me, and I had a good dump, Grade 1 on the Bristol – 'hard lumps like nuts'. Painfully slow movers, and a sure sign of dehydration. I had to really push, forcing them out one by one – which was a mistake, one should never push. In consequence my haemorrhoids were raging. Fortunately, Beth and Adrian were also sufferers of the itch that knows no shame, and a well-thumbed tube of Anusol was close at hand and quick to find. He applied it liberally and internally using the special applicator, which was a shrewd move – it brought its blessed relief on pronto. It also broke the silence. He joked that it was like the Napa Valley between my cheeks and that he'd never seen my grapes so swollen. It made me chuckle and the atmosphere between us lightened. I think we've turned a corner, me and him, we're getting on with each other much better now, and it's nice. I think we're friends again.

'What are you going to do now?' he said, with his big gloomy innocent eyes. 'Now that you're wanted?'

'I'm only wanted in the region,' I camply replied.

'Are we going to go on the run?' he asked, with an earnest and impish appeal.

'Hmmm…' I thought, a cheeky suggestion, but why not? This city is, after all, a sewer. Why not go on the run – get out into the country, smell the shit in the air?

'You'd need a disguise,' he said

'Yes, I would,' I said.

'You could dress up as Adrian and steal his car,' he spluttered, quick as a flash. He'd obviously been holding this thought for some time, and wanted to be credited with thinking of it first – so I let him think he had and replied, 'Ridiculous – I haven't driven in years.'

'It's like riding a bike,' he said.

'Absurd,' I said.

'Get back in the saddle,' he said. 'Head north.'

'Hmmm...' I pondered. Dress up as Adrian, steal his car, head north?... And then I remembered... Valerie lives up north. Valerie lives in Leeds – and I haven't seen Valerie in years, in seven years...

'Is it that long?' he said.

At least that long, I pondered. But why the hell not? Head north – see Val. Who knows, it might be fun.

A clean pair of boxer shorts, cotton socks, blue shirt, red silk tie and a rather smart, well-fitted, black suit from Hugo Boss. A pair of black brogues – a half a size too large, but nothing that an extra pair of socks and the odour-eaters from my shoes couldn't correct. A new watch, removed from Adrian's very rigid, blood-encrusted wrist – Ellesse, chunky stainless steel and good to a depth of two hundred meters, very reliable. Beth's spectacles – asexual wire-framed oval lenses, covered in blood but soon rinsed clean, wiped dry and slipped on. I looked very professional, trustworthy even, honest and a success. Nothing like the scabrous oaf now famous throughout the region for the Sudder Street Slaughter.

'You look like someone,' he said. 'Who is it?'

And we looked at me in the mirror and considered... He was right, I did look like someone, who was it?

'It's Tony Blair,' he blurted.

And he was right. I look just like Tony Blair. A slightly bruised, characterfully haggard, somewhat raffish, paranoid

Tony Blair... I admired myself, smiled and felt confident.

'You know who that makes you then, don't you?' I said, and he looked at me, glowering. 'That makes you Gordon Brown.' He rolled his tongue along the inside of his lower lip, smiled and looked bashful.

'And you know what he said, don't you?'

'What?'

'Better to die roaring like a lion than braying like a donkey.'

'Did he really say that?'

'No – but he did say that courage is not the absence of fear, it is the realization that some things are more important than safety.'

'Indeed.'

'A lesson Adrian might have learnt.'

'Yes.'

We smiled sagely, congratulated each other, and then went in search of the car keys. I found them in the pocket of a three-quarter-length macintosh hanging on the back of the hall-cupboard door. I slipped the mac on and took one last look around the flat. Adrian was lying with his face buried in the seat of the big white armchair, his legs splayed out behind him, blood everywhere. Beth was twisted beneath the duvet, her arms delicately crossed and her little hands folded into fists, her stomach split, and her pretty hazel eyes still staring... What have I done? I thought. What have I done...? And then other thoughts festered and started to seethe. On the mantelpiece were two photographs – one of Adrian and one of Beth, both of them smiling and looking happy. Those will be the photographs they'll put in the newspaper, I thought, beneath the headline: Two Found Dead in E5 Bloodbath. Yes, I pondered, that will be forever how Beth and Adrian are remembered – smiling, happy, and butchered... That is, of course, if they are remembered at all. But I'm sure they will be – they're the connected type. They'll each have a mother and father, each have brothers and sisters, each have friends and colleagues... They'll be missed and remembered... Their deaths are, after all, exceptional in their brutality and futility, so there's a chance they may make it onto the television. And then there'll be a wave of mawkish sympathy. Shrivelled bunches of daffodils bought at the local garage will be left on the pavement with misspelt messages of fond remembrance from people they never knew. Tears will be wept and kind words spoken. It will all be very sad...

And then I remembered the photograph they put in the papers of Emma – smiling, happy, and butchered... And I remembered an afternoon dredging a ditch. And I remembered the smell of damp, and a head, and a leg, and a foot, and an arm...

I turned the heating off, locked the door, pocketed their keys, slipped back into my flat, gathered some things, turned my heating off, locked my door and was gone.

As I exited the building my heart was racing.

'Be calm,' he said. 'Be confident, you're a professional. No-one's going to recognize you.'

'I've always been a head-turner,' I said. 'You know that.'

'Relax,' he said. 'You're disguised.' And then he started whistling. It was that tune again, that tune my father used to whistle. That cheery good-morning off-to-work whistle. I recognized it immediately, but this time – for the first time in a long time, the words sang along in my head...

> Mister Cellophane
> Should have been my name
> 'Cause you can look right through me
> Walk right by me
> And never know I'm there.

It made me wonder just what sort of a man my father was. What sordid horrors of his own did his life hide? That biscuit salesman for McVitie's... I was eleven when he died, on a beautiful summer's evening in 1977... I remember, for some time afterwards, feeling deeply aggrieved, and bitterly resentful. Not at Dad for having died, but at Mum for telling the mourners that his last words were: 'Never trust a garibaldi.' It got a good laugh and eased a lot of grief, but it was a lie. Mother wasn't even present when he died. His last words were: 'Oh fuck... please.' And then he made a terrible pitiful noise. A noise that signified intolerable and excruciating pain, caught gurgling in his throat. His body twisted and contorted. He held himself tightly, collapsed onto the lawn, looked at me with a terrible dread-filled anguish, reached out towards me, and then died... I let go of my kite and ran away from him, back into the house, and called for Mum... I didn't know what else to do.

The key ring told me I was looking for a Vauxhall Vectra. I didn't have any idea of what a Vauxhall Vectra looked like, but there were only three cars parked in the immediate vicinity – one was a dilapidated orange Beetle, the second a small black

Cinquecento with a Che Guevara bumper sticker and a Cornwall flag in the window, and the third was a dark-blue, middle-management-looking car – so I figured it had to be that one. I aimed the key at it and clicked the button, the car bleeped, flashed and snapped open. I got in and immediately felt safe and warm. The car was immaculate and smelt of an Alpine forest. It had air conditioning, a sun roof, airbags, a CD player, surround-sound speakers, a cup rack, four doors, a large boot, front and rear screen wipers, automatic windows, child locks, adjustable seating – it had it all. There was a button for everything. And he was right, it is like riding a bike – once you're back in the saddle, it all comes back to you. A bit of a bumpy start – super-sensitive brakes – but once I got a feel for them we were off – both arms up, hands at ten to two – mirror, signal, manoeuvring north. Destination: number 3, Kepler Grove, Leeds.

It was a slow uncertain sneak out of London, a nervous crawl onto the motorway, and then a mad dash north up the M1, stopping only once for a piss and a cup of coffee at the services just outside Leicester. Nobody paid me any mind – I was just another journeyman heading north.

The time was straight north and south as I pulled up outside Valerie's house. The daylight hours had returned to dark and the past returned to the present. My body was aching, my thoughts were teeming, seven years of separation were about to be undone. Seven years of kennelled gloom, hounding me and barking, yapping at my ankles, were about to be let loose.

I got out of the car and stretched. The evening air was a

bitter icy cold. Goose bumps, like frozen kisses, pimpled up and down, biting me all over, and an anxious shivering dread quivered within. I pulled my mac on and gathered it around me. I locked the car, it squawked and bleeped as if to say 'Good luck.' My thoughts fastened, my breathing equalled. I knew what I must do. As I lifted my finger to the doorbell, I noted that my hand was shaking.

I pressed the bell and waited...

Valerie always kept good time, she was very efficient with minutes. She liked time, it was a structure she could work with, make sense of and rely on. At six o'clock she would be sitting down to have her 'tea', as she liked to call it, being a good honest northern girl. Valerie always took her tea at six o'clock, she believed very firmly, almost to the point of high principle, in fixed eating times. It was how she controlled her bowels. She liked control. She became distracted and troubled if she ever lost control and didn't 'express', as she ever so politely put it, 'on time'.

'I'm not an iconoclast!' she'd say, smiling. It was our joke. 'I want to go first thing in the morning, not last thing at night.' And then we'd laugh and snuggle up beneath Egyptian cotton covers and make loving squeaking noises. But I digress...

A dark refracted shadow loomed behind the frosted glass. The door opened, and there she was... She had grown so old. And seemed to have shrunk. She looked thin and worn and used. Everything about her had fallen. Her hair line had retreated, her gums had receded, her skin was limp, pendulous and yellow... Life and time had worked their degenerate witchcraft.

'Yes?' she said.

And then looked at me. Nine seconds passed. Count them.

1

2

3

4

5

6

7

8

9

'Peter?' The penny dropped. Her little voice not quite believing.

A sad, pathetic smile inched its way sideways into my cheeks.

'What are you doing here?' she said – her face creasing and eyes widening.

'I've come to see you,' I heard myself nervously mumble. And then there was a pause. A twitching, bewildered, off-kilter incertitude was undoing her. She was confused. I could see her thinking... This hadn't been planned, there hadn't been a phone call first – no arrangements had been made – a line, letting her know, hadn't been dropped – this was unexpected, and all of a sudden, and out of the blue. She was unsure of how to react. What to think? What to do?... And a dark emotion bristled between us.

'You'd better come in,' she said, abandoning her discomfort to the safer formalities of procedural cliché, and showed me through into the 'lounge', as she liked to call it, where we stood, uneasily opposite one another, in the middle of the room, in complete silence, for exactly twenty-seven seconds.

Count them. And don't rush…

1
2
3
4
5
6
7
8
9
10
11
12
13
14
15
16
17
18
19
20
21
22
23
24
25
26
27

It was electrifying. Our breathing was at odds throughout.

The intense discomfort of being human, each uncertain of the other, the stark reality of our existence and the unalterable history between us, abruptly, and all of a sudden, squashed together in a confined space, jangling, stilted and irreconcilably at odds – after all those years. I can't describe it – but it was wonderful. It was so intense, such exquisite awkwardness… For twenty-seven seconds, a gluey sensual unease, binding us – and an urgent ticking, racing and harrying time… It was extraordinary. I felt profoundly alive… I can't explain it, but for all of its awfulness, I would have held that moment forever.

My eyes gave the room a rapid, glancing going-over. It was a small room, untouched by the Ikea sensation and full of cheap oversized traditional English MFI. A matching sofa and armchair in the old-fashioned chintzy second-hand style, a simple round wooden table with two chairs, a television and video and DVD player and satellite box, an electric fire with pine surround, a carriage clock, a few shelves, a few books – Mary Wesley, Catherine Cookson, Joanna Trollope – a bureau full of things – who on earth keeps a bureau these days? Some posters of art from galleries – National and Tate, touting good taste, in clipframes. A green-and-gold carpet, floral curtains, and in pride of place, above the fire, a portrait of Jesus Christ – the prophet son of carpenter Joseph. There he was in all his bearded glory, with his sacred heart, his bleeding palms, his crown of thorns, modern good looks and devout attendance. Everything was very neat. Everything very tidy. Everything in its place. And everything almost exactly as I had remembered it, as I had last seen it, seven years before. I'd been up on a reconciliation bid, which needless to say ended in tears. I arrived late, and it all went wrong from there. I can't be bothered to relate the tired details of that miserable encounter now, and anyway it's all irrelevant, all that is needed to say is that her last words to me then were: '*You* killed my child. It was *your* fault. *You* killed Emma.'

But we looked at each other now through much older and sadder eyes...

'I was just about to serve my tea,' she said, turning away and gesturing towards the kitchen. 'Have you eaten?'

My stomach rumbled, imploringly, right on cue. 'No,' I replied.

'It was only nothing but I can put some gravy on...' She knew she hadn't made sense but it didn't matter.

'Yes,' I said – her eyes returning to mine – 'that'd be nice.' And then we held a look and remembered... And then we looked away. There was something in that look that I didn't understand at the time – but picturing it now, as I write this, I can see there was something in it, something that should have told me, something I should have remembered, but had forgotten... But I digress... My eyes were darting – away from Valerie and into a shadow in the corner of the room, and then to the ceiling, and then to a photograph on a shelf of Emma fresh out of the bath, sat on her mother's knee, wrapped in a big thick towel. I didn't linger on it – I couldn't – I deliberately moved my eyes away from it quickly and onto another photograph of a woman I didn't recognize, standing in a blue cagoule in front of a red minibus, smiling and holding some rope. I remember I didn't understand the photograph, it had nothing to do with anything I knew or understood about Valerie, and it confused me. Who was this woman, I thought, and why was she holding a rope?

'Who's she?' I asked, unfolding my arms and pointing.

'Oh, that's Pat,' she said, nervously twisting the corners of her cardigan. 'She's a friend of mine, we go climbing.'

'Climbing?' I repeated, my eyebrows arching.

'Yes, I joined a club.' And then she splayed the fingers of her left hand, stretching them out, wide apart. It was a childish, anxious, edgy shadow move that she seemed to be quite unaware of making, but I noticed it.

Look at her, I thought, look at what's become of her, careworn, and worn out. She was dressed in a long brown Marks & Sparks cardigan, a black pleated skirt and thick black tights, ridiculous slippers, her hair scraped back and tied, her face unadorned, drawn and emaciated. She looked like a nun, which made me smile. Valerie had always wanted to be a nun. It was another of our jokes. I'd've loved to have been a nun, she'd declare – but I wanted a family – so what could I do? And then she'd kick her heels and flounce away, beaming silly girlish smiles... And you had a family too, didn't you, Val? But your family failed you. Your daughter was butchered and your husband lied and left you ... Your smiles are not so brazen now, are they?

I glanced at the carpenter's son, and then back at Emma and then back at Valerie... And then I realized I no longer knew anything about Valerie. She had changed, as all things must, and as all things do... We were strangers now, our lives no longer each other's. We existed in separation, as all humans must, and as all humans do. What we had shared was now nothing more than a few sorry chapters in an awful little story full of heartache, grief and dole. The arbitrary moments of rec-ollection, the absurd arrangement of words and the random druthers of detail, were now all that remained between us... This is all very obvious, I know, but the sudden realization of it affected me. I folded my arms. And then folded my arms again. The silence broke.

'Right, I'll put an extra sausage on. Why don't you sit down and make yourself at home?' Her last few words seemed to stick in her throat as she turned and disappeared into the kitchen. Make myself at home? I thought, slipping out of Adrian's mac, hanging it on the corner of the door and sitting down – my only home is Hell... I pondered for a moment, thinking of nothing, and then a sinister smile thinned my lips and a devil-may-care insouciance warmed.

'You know what's going to happen now, don't you?' he said, stepping out of the shadows. He'd been lurking in the corridor by the front door, listening to us the whole time.

'She's going to want to talk to you now,' he said, circling the room, and anxiously rubbing his hands. They were so cold.

'And you know what she's going to want to talk to you about, don't you?'

He was right. I glanced at Emma. A heavy dread churned in my guts.

'She's going to want to catch up. And you're going to have to talk to her.' He stopped and looked at me, meaningly, as if to let what he had just said sink in. I said nothing, put my eyes to the ground and pondered. 'You're going to have to tell her everything now...' he went on, shoulders slumped, neck twisting, heckling paranoid jibes. 'She's got her ways and she knows how to work them. She'll be on to you – she'll have you under the microscope, she's already got you in close-up – and she's going to want to know, and you're going to have to tell her. There'll be no getting away from it. She's already wondering what you're doing here, and she has every right to – she hasn't seen you in seven years – you've a lot to talk about, and she'll get it out of you – she'll start asking her questions – she likes to ask questions – asking is control, answering is chaos – '

And then he stopped, quite abruptly stopped, and held me – possessed – with a fierce and stern grimace. He was sweating. There was a pause. A long weighted pause. And then he said, very deliberately, he instructed me to 'Tell her everything… Tell her everything,' he hissed. 'Confess it all.'

My heart was beating, I was shaking. His face was close to mine, I could feel his breath, tickling the hairs in my nostrils. I could see the spittle on his gums, the tarnish on his teeth, the shine on his eyeballs. All the little lines, and little hairs. All the little details of his face.

'You won't be able to stop yourself,' he went on. 'You're going to spill your guts to her, Crumb, like a blubbering child, and have every dirty word of it off your chest. Let her ask her questions – she wants to know – give her answers… This is *your* Hell, Crumb, and now you'll make it hers…'

He squeezed the ends of his cold and bony fingers, stared at me, and sniggered. 'Bless me, Valerie, for I have sinned, it is seven years since my last confession…' The carpenter's son said nothing.

She bustled back into the room. She was wearing an apron and carrying two place mats, some cutlery and two napkins.

'I thought we'd eat in here,' she said, crossing to the round table in the alcove and laying two places.

'Is there anything I can do to help?' I asked.

'It's all right,' she said. 'It's all done now.'

And then she disappeared back into the kitchen, returning almost immediately with a bottle of cold white wine – Pinot Grigio – two glasses and a corkscrew, already inserted.

'Here,' she said, handing me the bottle. 'You can open that and pour us both a glass.' I took the bottle and corkscrew and she smiled. There it was again – something familiar, but forgotten... She kicked her heels and bustled back into the kitchen... I put the bottle between my knees and pulled the cork, poured myself a large glass and downed it in one and then refilled my glass and Valerie's.

It was all too reminiscent. Far too reminiscent. The sight of the cutlery froze me. I recognized it immediately. It had been given to us as a wedding present. The memory of that joyful afternoon, fifteen years before, freshly wed, opening presents, giggling and kissing, replayed in my mind. My heart swelled and stuck in my throat. I wanted to cry. We were once so happy, and so in love. I thought it would never end.

'How foolish,' he said. 'Do you remember what your response to this so-called present was on that so-called joyful afternoon?... You sneered at it and said, "What a cliché."'

He was right, I had mocked that fancy box of knives and forks and the vulgarity of its aspirant pretensions. Yes – and I had felt clever in doing so, but also ashamed. I remember how that little look of hurt furrowed Valerie's brow. That fearful look of pain she used to wear. The cutlery service was a present from her parents. And Valerie loved her parents.

They'll be good for dinner parties, she said, do you remember? She was always so positive, and so enthusiastic – so lively and animated. You loved her for it... Her belief in people, her faith in humankind and her urge to feed them all in a never-ending round of dinner parties. All the life she had in her. That lightness and verve – such energy – do you remember? Like a force of nature, you used to say – it was your joke, another of your miserable jokes – just a forty-watt light bulb me, you'd bleat, but she, she was the sun. Full of zip and sizzle – the happy unembarrassed truth of her... Now all gone... Yes, I pondered, the melancholy burden of reflection heavy and aching inside me, she had some snap all right, lots of doing... The thought made me smile. People coming round to eat, jollying and getting drunk, the house crackling with chatter... Whatever happened to all those people? Friends, we used to call them... I finished my wine, sat down, poured myself another and waited...

Valerie re-entered. She was carrying two large plates laden with sausages, mash and peas, all of it swimming in a thick dark gravy. It's a traditional English dish – sausages and mash ... S&M we used to call it. Not one of our jokes, more of a pastime, a sometime detour into sexual perversity... 'Do you swing?' I'd enquire, the routine well rehearsed. 'No,' she'd reply, 'I usually vote Labour!' 'Ah,' I'd conclude, comically licking my lips, 'a Fabian.' And then with a wolfish leer I'd pull her over my knee, giggling and wriggling coyly, as I yanked at her moist little knickers and spanked her... But that was all a very long time ago...

She placed the food in front of me and then sat down at a right angle next to me. We simultaneously reached for our napkins and our knees touched beneath the table. I took up my knife and fork and was about to tuck in when I noticed that Valerie was sitting with her eyes closed and her hands folded in her lap. Oh my God, I thought, she's saying grace. Her lips were silently thanking the Lord for what we were about to receive. She opened her eyes and blessed herself, glancing insinuations as her hand bounced judgement between the Father, Son and Holy Ghost. I felt awkward and godless and rashly started to bless myself, but then forgot halfway through which way round you do it, and felt inept and fraudulent and trodden on.

'It's all right,' she said, with a mean and bitter superiority, taking up her knife and fork and cutting the head off a sausage. 'You don't have to. I know you don't believe.' And then she shovelled and squashed her mash and peas into her sausage and onto her fork, brought it up to her mouth, and blew... Her lips were thin and grey and creased, puckered up into a tight little blow-hole, all the pink of Manon gone. Her tongue was darting, lizard-like, backwards and forwards, tentatively testing the temperature of her food. The memory of Emma, a toddler at the table being fed, returned to haunt, and a swollen amplified silence burped between us. I put my eyes to the ceiling and stared, pretending to be fascinated by the Artex swirls. The burdened prospect of polite conversation loomed...

'I put a bit of mustard with yours,' she said, merrily kicking off. I looked at my plate and saw a thick gelatinous dollop of mustard nestling between my peas and mash, and instantly felt sick.

135

'Is it Colman's?' I heard myself enquiring without knowing why.

'Of course,' she cheerily replied. 'I remembered how you liked your Colman's.'

And she was right. I did like Colman's. It was something I had completely forgotten – my fondness for mustard. Colman's traditional English mustard – none of that French muck, we used to joke. It made me smile. And then Valerie smiled, pleased with herself, and made a sweet little 'humph' noise.

'You're looking very well.' She went on, relaxing, settling in and taking a large swig on her wine.

I felt myself in Adrian's suit, tight, with sweating armpits, and made a noise that signified acknowledgement.

'How long have you been wearing glasses for?' she continued, her cold grey eyes enquiring. I put down my knife and fork and reached for Beth's lenses. Something else I had forgotten.

'Oh, they're just for driving,' I timidly replied, peeling them from my face and tucking them into my breast pocket. Valerie smiled wanly. There was a pause. I felt his breath on my neck.

'So what are you up to these days then?' she went on, taking another large swig on her wine.

'Oh,' I said, not knowing. 'I'm just... You know, I'm...' My mind was racing, sifting through lies.

'Are you back at work?'

'Erm, yes, I'm...'

'What are you doing?'

I stared at my plate. The silence fell. I felt a quickening tingle, shivering through me. And then I heard myself say,

'I sell tiles.'

I have absolutely no idea where it came it from.

'Oh.' She chirruped, somewhat boggled. 'Ceramics?'

'Yes.' I nodded shiftily.

'That's a bit of a departure.'

'Yes,' I said, and then paused to chew… Valerie emptied her glass and poured herself another.

'I could do with some new tiles in that bathroom.'

I didn't respond, just smiled feyly, moved some mash around my plate and pictured grouting, covered in mildew.

'Anyway,' I sighed, affecting a nonchalant normalness, 'how are things with you?' It's a standard middle-class conversational directive, but I timed it well, stressed the word you and gave it enough upward inflection to carry.

'Oh…' she said, as if flattered to have been asked. 'I'm back at the local primary…' There was a pause. She put down her knife and tucked a wayward strand of dark-dyed hair back behind her ear. 'It's nice, you know, with the kids…' And then she reached for her glass.

'Yes…' I growled, slowly, with thought. And then we both fell silent, and remembered Emma.

I remembered that day on the beach in Polzeath and the photograph I found in my pocket. I remembered her bucket and spade and her delighted, giggling squeals for 'Ice cream, ice cream!' And then I remembered that day spent dredging a ditch, and that smell of damp… I remembered her scattered pieces, mutilated, tortured, and chopped… And I remembered the torment and the sorrow and the rage… I stared at my sausages, hacked to pieces, their skin blistered, peeling and burnt… My breathing juddered, my chest began to shake and I realized I was crying.

Valerie turned and looked at me. There was an awkward pause of some length, and then I felt her hand reaching out to me, gently touching my arm. I turned to face her, and she cradled my hands tenderly in hers and held me. We looked at each other for a very long time. We didn't speak, there was no need, she understood, and a deep compassion shone in her eyes. I could hear my heart beating in the held stillness between us. My thoughts were reeling and jamming, stuck with tears and confusion… I felt quite out of myself, overcome and overwhelmed by memory… I crumpled inward, sobbing and helpless. Valerie's hands were tight around mine, her eyes searching deep into my soul. She brought my fingers to her lips and gently kissed their tips, and then she pulled me close into her arms, and held me.

'You're a good man Peter…' she breathily reassured.

'I am in Hell…' I moaned, baleful with woe. It was all very odd.

'I have prayed for this, Peter, and at last you have been delivered.' What was she talking about – had prayed for what? I pulled myself out of her embrace. She was smiling with such affectionate concern. Her hands were reaching and cupping my face, and then she leant in and gently kissed my mouth. My eyes were stinging red. I could smell the wine on her breath. I felt very confused.

'There is nothing covered, Peter, that shall not be revealed; and hid, that shall not be known.'

What on earth was happening? What on earth was she

talking about? I could feel my face contorting and twitching, the stuck gasps of broken sobs lurching in my chest. Her eyes were flickering backwards and forwards between mine, a pained, distraught affinity wrought between us.

'He torments me...' I whimpered, simpering on hysterically. 'He torments me... His evil is in me...'

'Cast him out, Peter. Cast the evil out. In God is love, Peter, find peace in God's love...' She fell to her knees with a gutsy resolve, pulling me down beside her. 'We must pray, Peter, we must pray together now, and cast the evil out.'

It was ridiculous and idiotic and humiliating. Valerie racing through an Our Father, warming up into a Hail Mary. Me on the floor beside her, snivelling, sobbing and gasping Amens... The carpenter's son looked down on us both but said nothing. He was wise to stay out of it. The other lurked in the doorway, frosty with contempt, watching me, and in such a pointed way ... It made me think of my mother, I couldn't help but picture her, standing in my bedroom doorway, holding that plate of chilled chocolate digestives. Me in my pyjamas weeping, Dad looking stern, stinking of pipe... I felt so embarrassed and ashamed. I struggled to my feet and collapsed back into my chair. Valerie remained kneeling on the floor in front of me, watching me, her left hand delicately placed on my right knee.

'I'm sorry,' I said, bumbling and sniffing, trying to pull myself together. 'I'm sorry... I shouldn't have come here.'

I tried to stand but Valerie wouldn't let me. She had both her hands on my legs, and was pawing me back into the seat.

'No,' she said. 'It's all right... I'm glad you've come...' And then she looked at me in that way again, full of forlorn appeal.

'I shouldn't have come here,' I stammered. 'I should go. I've got to go...' I tried to push her away.

'No – please, Peter...' she was pleading. 'Don't go... I'm glad you've come... Please, don't go Peter...' A look of naked desperation settled between her eyes. 'I've missed you, Peter... Please, don't go.'

I didn't know what to say.

'I've often thought of you,' She went on. 'Often wondered what you were up to, hoped that you were well... I've tried to get in touch with you but... ' Her sentence trailed away into silence... And then she looked at me, very earnestly and said, 'I have prayed for your return, Peter, and hoped that you would come. I have waited for you, Peter.'

And then she rested her head on my lap and wept. I looked down at her, her arms reaching up around my body, holding me, needing me, her chest pressed heaving against my legs, her face buried in my thigh, and her tears wetting my trousers... It was all so reminiscent. The sight of her, collapsed in my lap, clinging to me, and sobbing... just like Emma, bawling, and kicking and crying, protesting bedtime, holding me tight, not letting me go. I remembered how I calmed her, and hushed her, and stroked her hair. The tender, gentle affection a father shows his daughter. I placed my hand on Valerie's head and lovingly recalled those troubled bedtime moments... Shhh... Shhhh... Shhhh...

And then the worm turned... He moved through the shadows towards me, that thin, sinful, conspiratorial smirk twisting the length of his lips, and a raw emotional depravity stirred in my loins... My penis was throbbing, and she could feel it bulging in my trousers and pressing against her cheek. She lifted her head and looked at me. A silent unchecked insolent stare, and a dark brooding sentient corruption surged between us. She moved her hand and placed it over my erection and pressed. I did nothing to prevent her. She unbuckled my belt and unzipped my flies. Again, I did not stop her. My cock rose up, its purple end burning. She took it in her hand, controlling its eager twitches, considered it for a moment, probably to say grace, and then put her mouth on it. She sucked it and licked it, her tongue working it with a starved and wanton ardour. I felt a sordid delirious revulsion pulsate through me. Why on earth was she doing this, I thought – what desperate humiliating loneliness was motivating this? The awful truth of being human seemed suddenly very clear.

The carpenter's son put his eyes to the sky, and said nothing...

Afterwards, we lay on the floor, next to each other, in silence, not moving, just listening. Regret was quick to take advantage, seeping in between us and oiling its sticky misgivings. Valerie broke first. She got up, brushed herself down, straightened her skirt, crossed back to the table, took a large swig on her wine, picked up the plates, looked at me, sort of smiled, raised her chin and then disappeared back into the kitchen. I got up, put myself away, tucked myself in, and considered my position. I could hear taps running, filling a sink, and the muted tumble of pots and plates knocking and bumping. She's going to hide in the kitchen and do the washing up, I thought.

'Yes,' he said, 'Well, fair enough, why not? I would – after that carry-on... Wouldn't you? Huffing and puffing,

141

squirting your seed all over. Dear Christ, Crumb, what kind of an animal are you?'

I reached for my tobacco and started to roll a cigarette, but then suddenly remembered Valerie's extreme views on smoking, and how the fags had killed her father. She'll want me to go outside and smoke it, I thought.

'Perfect,' he said. 'And then you can fuck off. Say you're going for a fag and then just get back in the car and drive the fuck out of it. What are you doing here anyway? You've had your way with her – got things off your chest – now get the fuck out. Get back in the car and get the fuck out of it, Crumb.'

He was right. And then she entered. I turned sharply and guiltily blurted, 'I was just going to have a cigarette.'

'Oh…' she said

'I'll go outside,' I said, and stepped towards the door.

'Well… I mean, only if you think so.' And then she nervously edged her way further into the room towards me. 'You don't have to go out if it's just the one.'

The cunning bitch – trying to cut me off at the pass. She knows my game.

'No, it's all right, I don't mind,' I said, reaching for my mac.

'There's no need to take your coat,' she said, that look of desperate appeal lurching forward into her eyes.

'It's cold,' I said.

'Well, why don't you just stop in here and have it?'

'… I wouldn't mind the air,' I mumbled, carrying on, not listening to her, pulling the mac around me. 'I'll only be a minute.'

She was uncertain of what to do.

'You're not going to go, are you?'

I stopped. That forlorn helplessness was all about her.

'No,' I steadily reassured, placing my hands on her shoulders, leaning in and gently kissing the side of her mouth.

'I'll put the kettle on then, will I?' She was trying ever so hard to please. It was all so grim, and treacherous.

'Yes,' I said, opening the front door and stepping out. 'Put the kettle on, I'll be back in a minute.'

But we both knew I was lying. We both knew that the moment I closed that door behind me, I was closing it for good. Rotten lying liar.

I crossed to the car, it bleeped and snapped open. I got in, rolled a jazz cigarette, a strong one – a real old-fashioned banger – sparked her up and reflected on what had just passed. I felt such shame, the terrible grip of guilt was on me, tightening in my chest, and an awful grubby accountability was rubbing up inside. The feral depravity of it. The furtive desperation of it, and the sight of her sex – old, and bald, and yawning… Urgh – the thought of it sticks in my throat, and the taste of mustard repeats. Loneliness is an awful thing, but it's something we all have in common. I took a last long tug on my jazz and exhaled a huge plume of thick purple smoke. A man of evil conscience, Crumb – he cannot act well… I lowered the window, dropped the butt of jazz out, and let the smoke thin. My mind was swimming, my senses were dizzy, feelings and re-criminations running wild. I closed my eyes and stared into the darkness. I felt so tired. I just wanted it all to end… But I knew it wouldn't end, it will never end.

I opened my eyes and glanced back at the house. Valerie was

143

standing in the front-room window, watching me. She was just standing there, staring at me, and holding a tea towel. There she is, I thought – still my wife – still the mother of my child, and still the only woman I have ever really loved. And yet none of it makes any sense. I turned the key in the ignition, found first gear and then paused for a moment to give Valerie one last look. It was that look you've grown accustomed to me giving, that distant look of cold disdain – detached sorrowful disdain, remote and broken, I've perfected it.

Valerie's face mournfully broke into a smile, rueful but accepting. She lifted her hand to her shoulder, splayed her fingers wide in that childish way, such small and pretty hands, gave a little wave, made a 'write to me' gesture, paused for a moment, and then stepped back into the shadows and drew the curtains. I indicated east, and was gone.

It is now nearly midnight. I am sitting writing this in the darkened corner of a car park on an industrial estate somewhere on the outskirts of Leeds. It has been a long day... And I am tired ... so tired. Bach is on the radio, English suites, numbers 2, 4 and 5... He's in the back doing one of his drawings. I'm staring, trying to forget, hoping soon to sleep.

# FRIDAY

Last night I dreamt of Hell, and the guilty man that God forgot. Now it is morning, and the bad day has broken.

I should have booked myself into a hotel. Hiding all night in the darkened corner of a car park, it's animal behaviour – I don't know what I was thinking. But then I wasn't thinking – that was the trouble – he was – racing through thoughts – remembering. You know how he loves to recall – give him an evening and he'll be at it all night, digging things up that are all but forgotten, regurgitating details – all the little bits of in-between, thoughts about thoughts, and the guilty man… The guilty man that God forgot. Remember him? I remember him. How could I forget him, after what he did? You don't forget something like that in a hurry – oh no, it stays with you – it keeps you up all night, knowing that he's out there – going unnoticed – ambling on, up and down, to and fro – looking, seeing and thinking. You know the sort. The guilty man that God forgot… Yes – I remember him all right. How he used to torment me – worse than this one, I can tell you, much worse. All the evil things he did, you couldn't possibly imagine, but I saw, I saw with mine own eyes, as they like to say in certain circles. How he got away with it I'll never understand. Never caught, never brought to book. He has the luck of the devil that one – the kind of luck we'd all like. But he hates it, it rips at him – that he was forgotten. He wants to be caught, wants to be brought to book. In a noble way he wants to be counted. But he was forgotten, and if there is one thing he cannot stand, it is being forgotten. But forgotten he is, leaving me to remember…

And I do remember... I remember sad thoughts that are never happy... And I remember you...

But I digress... I feel very distracted this morning, my thoughts are scattered. As I said, it was a troubled night, I dreamt of Hell, and a badger, and now the bad day has broken.

# The Dream of Hell

I was ten years old. My father was leading me. Space was confined. The ceiling was low. I felt very afraid. He was walking so quickly, I couldn't keep up. The carpet was old and worn and threadbare. My feet kept catching and tripping on the torn strands, stumbling and burning my knees – they were bleeding. I was wearing shorts. I stumbled again, and hurt again. I was starting to cry.

'Not in that one. Not in that one.' He kept repeating it. His rasping nasal twang rising with exasperated irritation. He stopped and turned and looked at me, looked down at me, as I looked up, my socks around my ankles. There was no mistaking him – tall and thin, towering above me. He smiled and showed me his teeth. They were Dad's teeth all right. No mistaking those gums.

'This is your room,' he said, and then he turned and opened a door.

'In you go,' he said. 'They'll never find you in here.'

The room was dark and cold and stank of a moist sickly sweetness. There was no furniture, just a dirty stained mattress flopped on the cold stone floor in a corner.

'Come on now,' he commanded. 'No arguments – get into bed.' I didn't disobey. I walked to the middle of the room and slowly started to undress. He watched me. I removed my clothes very slowly, deliberately folding each piece by piece and placing them in a neat and tidy pile. First my jumper, shirt and shoes, then my shorts and socks, then my vest, and then my underpants… And then naked, ten years old, my little white limbs peeled clean, goose-pimpled and shivering. I remember a feeling of terrible dread. I knew that something awful was about to happen, something I couldn't control or stop. Troubled vibrations tickled my perineum.

'Lie down,' he said. I didn't disobey. I pulled the mattress flat, lay down and kept perfectly still. He leant forward over me, his face close to mine. His breath was of the kidney. I thought he was going to kiss me, but he didn't, he whispered, 'Lie perfectly still, and try not to breathe.' And then he was gone…

I closed my eyes, my heart was beating, I felt again the certainty of something savage about to unfold… And then it began. There was a noise, I opened my eyes… The badger. I cannot describe the degree of terror I felt at the sight of that hideous badger. As fat and as large as a circus dwarf, and black and filthy. Its thick fur covered in a greasy sap, and smeared with a sticky foulness – its twisted black claws scarring the floor – its snout, long and bristling with spiky hairs – its mouth slavering repugnant juices, its teeth, broken, chipped and razor sharp – and its eyes – a diseased yellow, stung with a poisonous red surround. It shuffled slowly towards me, licking and smelling the air. I took my father's advice and lay perfectly still and tried not to breathe. But it was no use. The badger knew, and was on me. My blood ran cold. My heart was pounding. I wanted to scream. He was on me, tonguing and sniffing and licking and scratching, his claws tearing at my flesh. I was bleeding. The weight of him on top of me, greasy and stinking, slavering juices – I could take it no more, I had to breathe – I gasped a huge gulp of air – but it was a mistake – the moment my lips parted he rammed his snout down into my gullet, choking me, forcing his head down into my mouth, his teeth biting and ripping through my throat, clawing into me, chewing his way through me, eating his way into me…

And then I woke… Rockall, Malin, German Bight… Such confusion, freezing cold, peering bleary-eyed about me… The time past south, south-east… Urgh, these wretched dreams, damned subconscious intrusions, fiddling with me in the dead of night. Make of them what you will… It is morning now, and the bad day has broken… And I am, as we say in England, fucking knackered.

And it's a horrible morning, overcast, wet and grey. A miserable northern day, full of aching limbs and stiff joints. Troubled thoughts to follow…

Something bad is going to happen today, something very bad, I can feel it…

There are humans everywhere, full of frenzied direct attending, this way and that. Onward Christian soldiers, marching as to work… and that righteous little weasel John Humphrys is at it again on the radio, eloquently working his wit, peddling his cheap opinions. The vain conceited villainy of the man, and those awful New Labour excusers. One twitters this way, and then the other twitters that. The everyday hula of opinion and point, spat back and forth between a monkey and a clown. One says to the other, and then the other says the same. Gobbling edible facts in easy-to-swallow bite-sized chunks, and all of it washed down with the sour swill of statistics. A live unscripted two-way, they call it. Pompous little

Englanders. Stupid humans and their molested opinions, endlessly repeated... And a woman called Margaret Dugdale – a
real Albion eccentric this one – Margaret, desperate to see a
dentist but unable to find one, took a pair of pliers to her
mouth and forcibly ripped her own teeth from her gums,
bloodily but boldly tearing them out, one by one. The mad old
sow then popped them all into an envelope and sent them to
the Home Secretary... Can you imagine? Toothless from
Tunbridge Wells! The mad bitch.

North by north-west.

Breakfast, greedily gobbled down at the hotel du ponce. I was served by a charming Albanian waitress called Malgazorta. She brought me my eggs exactly as ordered, no funny business, and I ate them all up without incident. Sipped my coffee and smoked a cigarette. It was charming, and so civilized to find somewhere that still accommodates smokers. I am feeling calmer now, and much more even… The day is up and running and I have had my dump – Grade 4 on the Bristol this morning: 'sausage with smooth surface'. It was like Frank Bruno's arm – my health returns. Whilst in the khazi I took the opportunity to spruce myself up. I fear my man-of-mode transformation is starting to wear thin. I'm starting to look a bit crumpled, and shadowy – wolfish even, heads are starting to turn again. I gave my face a good clean, combed my hair, straightened my tie, glasses on… I'll pass, for now, and our adventure can continue.

I am now sat back in the lounge, sipping another latte, smoking another cigarette, writing this and contemplating the day. The slow drip of what to do? There is a newspaper lying folded face down in front of me, but I can't be bothered with it yet. The thought of what horror it may deliver is too much – it's far too early in the day to start that carry-on. And I know it's going to be a bad day, so not yet… The time is south by north-west. I'm going to go and talk to the woman at reception.

I think I knew… if I'm honest. I think I knew then. I mean, the moment of first gleaning, I think it came as I walked towards you… I think I knew then, I can't be certain – I didn't pay it any mind – it was a fleeting thing, caught for less than a second, and then gone – but I think I knew then. You see, when I say that the newspaper was folded face down, and that I didn't yet want to see the headline, didn't yet want to be inculcated in whatever gruesome story the day had to herald – well, the truth is, I'm lying. You see, I had seen the headline. There were other newspapers, not folded face down, but folded face up. And so you see, I had seen the headline. And so you see, I knew, as I walked towards you – I knew...

Your name was Janice. You were wearing a name badge. You were a clean and well-presented woman, upright, polite and courteous. You had the sanitary air of a woman clean-flushed, and were dressed in a smart blue skirted suit, with black tights that showed off your nimble ankles, and feet in third position. Your hands were held politely in front of you, waiting to attend. You were about forty-five, slightly rubber-looking, with red lips that smiled.

'Can I help you, sir?' Those were your first words to me, Janice. Your voice was light and gently enquiring, your northern tones soft and warmly including.

'Yes,' I said, all formal, southern, educated and posh-toned. 'I was wondering if you could advise me...' – pausing for a beat to give weight to my enquiry, your head tilting, lips together. 'I've got a free day and I was just wondering if you knew of anything of any interest to do, or see, as it were, in Leeds, whilst I'm up here?'

And then for some reason I put my hand on my hip and rather ostentatiously raised my eyebrows, do you remember? You looked at me – a cream-faced loon with his eyes open round, full of innocent enquiry. I plopped them, gazing into yours and smiled. He is legion, I thought – honestly – the disarming charmer.

'Well, yes, there's lots of interesting things, let's see… What sort of thing is it you were looking for?' You blushed a little, didn't you?

'Well, I don't know,' I stammered, diffident and raffish.

'There's the theatre… D'you want me to check and see what's on?'

'Yes, that's probably not until this evening though –'

'Oh right – it's something for today, is it, you were looking for?'

'Yes.'

'P'r'aps they have a matinee?'

'Yes. On a Friday?'

'Should I see the times?' You were very professional, Janice.

'Is there anything else?' I said – do you remember? 'I'm not sure the theatre's really my bag – I find it all a little embarrassing.'

'I know what you mean,' you said, and then we both smiled, conspirators together – do you remember?

'Well, if it's shopping you're interested in –'

'Oh no, no,' I said, stopping you immediately. 'I can't stand shopping, or shoppers, they make me sweat.' I was overplaying it, I know.

'Oh,' you said, all Yorkshire jolly, 'just like my ex.' And then we smiled again, Janice, and I almost laughed, do you remember? You were flirting, Janice.

'Well, if it's something more cultural you were looking for, there're some nice walks, or what about a museum or an art gallery?'

156

I looked very blank, didn't I? The truth is, I didn't want to do anything. I was killing time Janice, avoiding the headline… Sniffing you out, Janice.

'Let me fetch you a leaflet,' you said.

It all sounded so dull – museums, galleries, walks, shopping, theatres, culture… You handed me a selection of flyers and leaflets and bid me, 'Have a look through that lot – if anything interests, I'll give them a call and see what they've got on.'

I shuffled back into the lounge and ordered another latte. Malgazorta busied. I leafed through the leaflets. All were as expected, the only one of any interest was for the Thackray Medical Museum: *From the horrors of the Victorian operating theatres to the wonders of modern surgery, the Thackray Museum's galleries, collection and interactive displays bring to life the history of health and disease, treatment and cures, medical discoveries, equipment and technology. Admission charged. Concessions available. 2 miles from city centre.*

Hmm… He pondered. Would going show malice aforethought?

The newspaper waited. There was no putting it off. I glanced back at you over in reception, do you remember? You caught my eye, your lips split and creases broke… I knew it would be you… And that made me happy. I felt reassured, glad that it was you, but also sad that it was you, that it was going to be you. The time was north by north-north-west. I paused for a moment and considered my conscience – it was totally inactive, both disinterested and uninterested. I reached for the newspaper, merely going through the motions. The headline, I already knew:

# WOMAN'S BODY FOUND IN BIN BAG

I thought of Emma and the guilty man.

And then I walked Janice, I walked all over, and I couldn't get you out of my mind – your lips, your gentle tones, warmly including, and your feet in third position, waiting to attend. You said, 'Enjoy yourself' – do you remember? And I smiled and said thank you. There wasn't hatred in your eyes then, Janice. You waved to me, happy to have been of service, and I waved back. There you were, Janice, alone, loitering in the empty corridors of my mind, playing with my memories, unattended. It was a foolish thing to do, Janice, my memories are not happy, they're grumbling, miserable and sorry – no-one should ever know of them… I tried to find another Janice, I kept saying to him, What about this one? What about that one? But he was having none of it. There was a fat one, with child, lumbering, lard-arsed, in the way, utterly useless, utterly stupid – no good to anyone – I said to him, What about her? I worked myself up into a rage over that fat one, Janice – and it was for you that I did it – I baited rage upon hatred and, let me be frank, murderous intent on that fat one, Janice, and her retard pant-crapping child, the stinking little shit. I can honestly say that I'd have taken great pleasure in sorting those two out – I'd've swung for the pair of them, as they say in certain circles – once bitten, going to be bitten again – but I'd've done it to keep you out of it, Janice. But no, he was having none of it. There was an old man – an old man even, an elderly – he could hardly walk. Doddering git, I heard him mutter – I thought I had him – but no, he wouldn't say boo to a goose, would he? I followed that bastard for miles, Janice, until my insteps were aching – all the way up the Headrow, onto a bus – I thought I'd convinced him, I was sure he'd agreed – but I told you, he's a conniving one, you can never second-guess him, he's a liar, a scheming pretender, and he'd decided. He'd set his heart on you, and that was that. That was that. There was no stopping him.

I got off the bus and there I was at the Thackray. Can you imagine, Janice? – with a headline like today's, my history and your feet. My blood ran cold, Janice – I can't describe it… He kept imagining you, Janice – on the operating table, tied to a gurney, screaming. All those tools, those instruments – his imagination was running wild, he was salivating, actually salivating – and licking my lips, which are now starting to chap, and I hate chapped lips. And I have to say, Janice, also, that the security at the Thackray Museum is absolutely appalling. It is an utter disgrace – in these terror-filled times one should not be able to steal, with ease, three scalpels of varying size, a small but very vicious-looking saw and a long thin Victorian knife, thought to be the type used by Jack the Ripper, ideal for fast amputation. And to steal them with such ease – that's what's so outrageous, that he could steal them with such ease. Nobody was there, nobody was watching – there wasn't even CCTV. Just me and him and you and my imagination – can you imagine, Janice? – all those tools, all those instruments, you wouldn't believe it.

He picked them up, Janice, and considered them. He held them in his hands – between his fingers – pretended to use them – and then quite casually wrapped them in his handkerchief and tucked them into my pocket. I was dumbstruck – the casual gall! And he could have taken a lot more, he could have filled a suitcase, Janice. Clamps, saws, drills – my God, Janice, you can't imagine the hardware available to these medicine men nowadays. They've got it all – the places they can go – and the tools they use to get there – my God, Janice, some things quicken when the devil drives – and the complexity of his mischief is beyond imagining, I can't tell you. These are the tools of the trade, he said, quite gleefully – these are the tools that man must have used… That guilty man, Janice, that guilty man that God forgot… I felt a long and terrible cold run through me when he said that, Janice. I felt a terrible evil inside me, turning, and I feared for you, Janice. I feared for you.

Do you remember when I came back just after lunch and you were finishing your shift? It was fate, you see. If I'd arrived a minute later I'd have missed you – you'd have gone and that would have been that. But there you were, putting your coat on and saying goodbye to your colleague Ray. You saw me and asked me how my morning had been – and when I told you, you seemed genuinely interested. Your eyes were open round and your head was angled, heedfully attending – I felt like a little boy telling his mummy how his first day at school had been, and I liked that feeling, Janice. But then you did something I didn't like. You turned and looked at Ray – you thought I couldn't see you, but I could see you, reflected in the mirror – I saw you lift your eyebrows and raise your eyes to Heaven, and I know what that look means, Janice, and I don't like it. It made me feel silly – and laughed at – the butt of some private joke, and I didn't like it, Janice, I didn't like it at all. I understand why you pulled such an expression – Ray is obviously a homosexual, I believe a lot of them work in the hospitality trade – and I know how they like to gossip and mock, Janice, they're a poisonous breed – 'marginales', as they say in France – and not to be trusted... But I digress...

I loitered, Janice, unobserved, and watched you leave, and then I followed you. He loves following people, Janice, he's known for it, and very good at it – he's at it all the time, and he followed you all over, Janice, watching you, window-licking your way through town and then stopping for a coffee... I watched you for some time, Janice, but you didn't see me. I wanted you to see me. I wanted you to look up and say, 'Oh hello again.'

But you didn't. If only you had, everything would have been different. I'd've joined you for a coffee, and we could have chatted and got to know each other and become friends. And then everything would have been different. But you didn't see me – you steadfastly refused to see me – kept your eyes to yourself and wilfully looked the other way. I was sitting only feet away from you, Janice. I could smell you. But you didn't want to see me, did you? You knew I was there, didn't you, Janice? But you didn't want to say hello, you didn't want to engage me in conversation – you didn't want anything to do with me – I thought you were a kind one, but you're not, and I see that now, Janice. And to think – there I was – imagining you and I, together, Janice, in a field, high on a hill, somewhere in the Chilterns, having a picnic. A picnic, no less – I should tell you, Janice, that I have never had a picnic with anyone, ever, so you can imagine the specialness of the occasion. You and I together, lying on a blanket, drinking champagne, me dressed in a bright white suit, feeding you ripe cherries. You with your naked toes, painted red, wiggling their way out of an old pair of mules, and your bottom pressed tight into a white cotton skirt. A beautiful view spread out on a beautiful day. On a silent day full of sunshine – yellow and red and blue and white, lilac and pink and still… the birds whistling in the distance, chirruping kisses. And you and I at ease beneath the boughs of an old oak, the gentle riffle of the wind through leaves…

Oh, what a lovely day that would be, Janice… We would talk, Janice, slowly, and openly, and honestly to one another. You would tell me all about yourself, all about your life – your marriage failing, your father's death, your feelings of regret, isolation and loneliness – and I would listen to you, Janice, and let you in – I would feel your unhappiness, and share with you some simple understanding, and want to ease your pain. I would tell you all about Valerie and Emma – and you would listen, and let me in – we would hold a silent look and not say anything – and then, perhaps, you might kiss me. What a lovely day that would be, Janice… A special day… I would hold your hand and look into your eyes, and you might, for a moment, all of a sudden, quite taken by surprise, think that I was about to propose to you, and a nervous excited feeling would tickle in your tummy and a breathless enquiring would burst in your eyes, and then I would tell you… I would tell you the rest of it, all the other things… All the awful things… And then your eyes would turn away and weep. And we would both weep… And then you would stop holding my hand, and you would look at me with an expression I wouldn't understand… And a fat ripe cherry would get squashed beneath your thigh and its red juices would bleed into your white cotton skirt…

But I digress… You finished your coffee and stubbed out your fag, got up and moseyed on… I watched you, I watched

166

you until you had almost disappeared, for a moment I thought you were going to get away – but then I got up and followed you… And I followed you all the way home, Janice. All the way back to 129, Warwick Way… And when I rang your doorbell, and you answered the door, you looked ever so surprised. It just hadn't occurred to you, had it? But the moment you saw me, standing there, smiling at you, at half past four in the after-noon – that cream-faced loon – south by south-west… Well, you knew then, didn't you, Janice? You knew… Your first in-stinct was to close the door and call the police, wasn't it, Janice? But those damned false manners of yours got in the way, just like Adrian – and you had to say hello, didn't you, Janice, those damned red lips of yours had to smile and those damned northern tones include… And that was all it took, Janice.

'Hello,' I said, rather too eagerly, I admit.

'What are you doing here?' you said.

'I'm here to see you,' I said

'What do you mean?' you said.

'Can I come in?' I said.

'No –' you said. But you're not big and strong, Janice, and I am. And all it takes is will, and a hand on the door, and a push hard enough to hit you and knock you backwards onto the floor, and then I can enter your house with ease, Janice, and calmly close the front door behind me. And now I'm in your home, and you're on the floor in front of me, Janice, and you're afraid – do you remember? You were panicking, Janice – in fear for your life. You've seen those programmes, you've read the papers – the worst-case scenario was chasing you through the house, screaming – but you see, I've seen it all before, Janice, I've heard these pleas – please, please – before, Janice. Remember Beth? She played a clever game… Silent to the end. She even ate the scone… But I digress…

I'm sorry that I had to hit you, Janice. I am aware that the brutality and ferocity of my attack upon you was ridiculously disproportionate to your attack upon me when you tried to escape – but one must be unequivocal in these matters and ruthlessly decisive. If I broke your arm, Janice, it was only to ensure that I wouldn't have to break your legs. I don't blame you for trying to escape, Janice – I commend you for it – you had some fight in you, Janice, most don't. But you must understand, from my point of view, I needed to subdue you – and I know from my own experience that a little bit of a fisting and a soft-soled shoeing never really hurt anyone – and as it was my intention from the outset to kill you – to dismember you – to put the bits and pieces of you into a bin liner and then throw you out with the rubbish – well… Who cares, Janice? In time your wounds will heal, in time the bruises fade – in time you won't wake in the night screaming, in time the horror and the terror, this evil and tonight, will all be gone. That's what they'll tell you – but it isn't true, Janice, it won't end, it doesn't ever end. The headline tomorrow will be the same as today's – and the same as the day after that – all will be repeated and endlessly regurgitated, round and round it rolls, Janice, in the swill it rolls, ever on, and on, and on… Once bitten, going to be bitten again… Your end was met, Janice, and what an awful end it was. This is what he did to you, Janice – this is what he did to you, and did to her, Janice, and did to me – that guilty man that God forgot. This is what he did – he beat her, Janice, just as I beat you, with his fists he beat her – and let me assure you there was nothing nice about it, Janice – it hurt – it was wild and vicious and messy and uncontrolled and savage and brutal and nasty. But it subdued her, Janice – just as it subdued you – and then he broke her arm, Janice. Just as I broke your arm. He broke her arm at its elbow, Janice, he stamped on it and snapped it, just as I... And just as I, he made sure not to kill, Janice. He had plenty more in store – that guilty man. It wasn't meant to be forgotten, Janice – he wanted the world to know. He stripped her naked, Janice... She was five years old... You, you were much older, much heavier, much harder to drag upstairs, much harder to dump in the bath. Imagine, Janice – if you can imagine – imagine him tying a cord tight around your ankles and then hoisting your legs high into the air. Picture yourself, Janice – your body naked, broken, black and beaten, your feet tied and bound to the shower fitting, your body slumped awkwardly and shamefully, an abused carcass, dangling upside down into the bath – all your blood rushing to your head – you were purple. Imagine that if you can, Janice... And now imagine, if you can, Janice, a five-year-old girl in the same predicament... Ponder that thought, Janice, hold that picture... For that is what he did, Janice – that is what he did to her – as I have done to you – and God forgot, Janice. God forgot ... But I don't forget – I remember – I'm very good at memory. I remember how he slit her throat, Janice, and drained her. I watched with mine own eyes, Janice, as he pulled that scalpel from my pocket and drew its blade across your throat. I saw with mine own eyes, Janice, your blood spill, and your life conclude… That is what he did, Janice – that guilty man that God forgot, he did it to her – and now I have done it to you… God is in his Heaven, on the right side and the left – the Father, Son and Holy Ghost, blithely unaware. But I remember, Janice – I will not forget – I remember… As I remember her… five years old, severed and drained like a halal chicken.

I left you to hang for an hour or two, Janice, came downstairs and unpacked the shopping, put everything away and then put that chicken-and-leek pie in the oven. It was delicious. I boiled some peas and made some gravy, sat at the kitchen table and ate it in reverent silence. And then I retired to the living room and watched the news and smoked a cigarette. I hope you don't mind, Janice, but I used that ornamental plate from Alicante as an ashtray.

The news, both national and local, was packed full with horror, but none of it mine. The lead story was about the woman found in a bin bag. There'll be more of that story tomorrow, Janice, when they find you… And then that story was followed by another equally horrifying story involving the abduction and murder of a little boy in Norwich. I can't remember his name but he was taken from his back garden by a ten-year-old girl who walked him into the woods, where her eleven-, twelve- and thirteen-year-old lynch mob were waiting. They tied a noose around the little boy's neck and then hanged him. And then that story was followed by a story about a little African girl, I can't remember her name either. She'd been sent to live with her aunt in England. Sadly her aunt believed that the little girl was possessed by devils – so the aunt took the little girl to a priest, who beat her and kicked her and whipped her, and rubbed chillies into her eyes, and stubbed cigarettes out on her skin, and broke her ribs, and cut her flesh with a knife heated to red-hot temperatures. And he did it all in the name of God with the full consent of the little girl's aunt... And then that story was followed by a story about two schoolgirls, one aged fifteen and one aged sixteen, again I can't remember their names but they were taken by five men, I think from Eastern Europe, to a flat, where they were held for two days, drugged and repeatedly gang raped. The five men then shot the two girls and dumped their bodies, in the dead of night, in a thicket of trees by the side of the road. And then that story was followed by another story about another pretty Asian girl – just like the one I knew, but not the one I knew, another one, a different one, last seen buying a jumper at TK Maxx. She suffered a terrible end. And then that story was followed by a rather amusing story about an elephant that had escaped from a zoo in China and gone on the rampage – the whole hilarious episode had been caught on camera and put to music. I have to admit it was very funny, and did make me laugh... And then came news of the weather – what today's weather had been, cold and grey and wet – and what tomorrow's weather would be, cold and grey and wet – but they presented it brightly and very cheerfully... I smoked a jazz cigarette and drew a picture. Then I sat in silence for a time and listened to the shuffling noises behind the wall and watched a fly buzzing and crashing into the window. Then I went back upstairs and stripped myself naked. I hope you don't mind, Janice, but I didn't want to get my clothes dirty, so I removed them, piece by piece, and folded them neatly into a tidy pile. It made me think of the badger... I entered the bathroom, the three scalpels, the knife and the saw that he'd stolen from the Thackray in one hand, and a roll of bin bags in the other. I closed the door behind me and set about my work. First I removed your head Janice, it was a textbook dissection. I held it aloft in front of me, gripping you by your hair, and I thought of Robespierre and Jacques Chirac – I heard myself saying, 'Il faux que la France dise – Non!' It made me chuckle and the vibrations in my arm made your head rotate and you sort of jiggled round and looked at me. It was eerie. You looked like John the Baptist in that ridiculous painting by Caravaggio. Quite gruesome. I bagged you quickly and then set to work removing your right arm – the broken arm – and then your left arm. Taking your arms off was the most fearful part of the whole operation. The way they kept lolloping around me and grabbing at me as I hacked away at your shoulder, viciously paring the flesh back to the bone. Your fingers kept catching in my hair – I couldn't bear it – I became exasperated and angry and virtually ripped your left arm off, ripped it off at the shoulder like a married man rips the wing off a Sunday roast chicken. I dropped the saw, grabbed your arm by the wrist with both hands, put my foot on your torso and yanked – violently. I was panicking, Janice. There was a fear in me – important to note it. And I have to say that I don't like arms, they're a troublesome, dangerous limb – best kept out of reach... Anyway, once I'd got them off, I bagged them quickly – straight in with your head. And then I remember I held the bag open and just stared into it. It was a ghastly, horrifying sight – your severed head, that tortured rent expression, and your arms, twisted and reaching. I couldn't tie the bag up quickly enough – fumbling as I did so – your arms poking and elbowing the sides – your fingers catching in the knot – it was like you were trying to claw your way back out – and the weight of your head… and that look – it was awful… And then the sight of your remains left hanging – your torso and legs, draining. One should never have to see such a sight… I cut you down and laid you out in the bath and then set about removing your legs. It took forever. Slicing deep into your thigh from your crotch up to your hip – it's no good being prudish, you have to get stuck in – get your hands dirty, get your fingers in – you have to hold the flesh apart and grapple with it and wrestle it. It takes effort and strength – you sweat, and as you sweat you know you're never going to forget it – it's exhausting and sapping and the blood is indelible, the stink of it permanent, the feel unerasable and the fact of it unalterable and horrible, horrible, and horrible… But I got it done… and got them off. And then chopped them up into three manageable pieces – off at the knees and the ankle… I have to say legs are an utterly ridiculous limb – they looked bigger off you than on you. They were absurdly long and cumbersome – they just looked daft. It made me think of Max Wall and Groucho Marx and John Cleese and funny walks… I put your calves and thighs in one bag and then was going to put your feet into another, but decided to leave them, sat on top of the toilet in third position – as a sort of sick joke. I couldn't help imagining Charlie Chaplin sticking two forks into them and then improvising a comic dance with them. It was beautiful and most memorable, but very sad and quite macabre… But I digress… I bagged the rest of you and then sat on the edge of the bath, exhausted and shaken. I was covered in blood. Everything was covered in blood, and there were little pieces of you everywhere – the off-cuts – it was disgusting… I stared at the three bin bags – your head and arms in one, your thighs and calves in another and your torso in a third, and I thought… What was the point of that?

I gave the bath a good clean and mopped up as much of the mess as I could, flushed some bits down the toilet, and then had a shower. I gave myself a good lathering and then got into your bathrobe, it was a bit small but quite comfy. I went into your bedroom and lay on your bed – everything was so white and fluffy, it calmed me and I reflected for a moment, and thought about what I had done, not only to you, Janice, but to Valerie, and Beth, and Adrian, and that girl, and her mum, and Milka, and Paul and Dan and Dave and Dieter. I thought about them all… and Emma, and the guilty man, and him and me… the grubby struggle of life, the lies and delusion, the vanity and futility of it all, and the gratuitous evil of it all… I felt deeply ashamed, and deeply revolted… And then I was sick – quite violently – I felt it coming on, the nausea, and was going to dash back into the bathroom, but I just couldn't face it, so I opened the top drawer of your dresser and spewed into that – all over your bras and knickers – the cheesy undigested remains of that chicken-and-leek pie, chundered up all over your smalls. It was revolting. I was sweating and shaking like a dog, shivering and retching. I think it's fair to say that I was having some sort of turn. A fit. I didn't know what was happening, so I lay on the floor… lay perfectly still, and tried not to breathe… After a time, I can't say how long, I remember I heard, somewhere in the distance – I heard an elephant scream – trumpeting rage…

It was a magical sound that spurred me on… I got up, pulled myself together, gathered my clothes, got dressed and gave the house a nervous going-over. I collected the bags from the bathroom and put each bag inside another bag, and then brought them all downstairs and lined them up by the front door. I wrapped the scalpels, knife and saw inside your bathrobe and then put them in the freezer compartment of the fridge. I then found your purse and stole sixty-five pounds, found your mobile and turned it off, and then I gave the house a second nervous going-over – checked I hadn't left anything, turned all the lights off, opened the front door and peered out into the street. The night air was so cold. My breath shimmered. All was quiet. I put the bags out for the bin men, quietly closed the front door behind me, pulled my mac tight, and was gone.

I am now back in the car, the time past south by north-north-east.

I have had enough, and am going home. Home to face the music, and dance.

# SATURDAY

It was a long drive south, up all night listening to him chattering nonsense about the police, babbling about being caught – leaving clues and fingerprints. I want them to catch me, I want to be caught – he kept repeating it, like a mantra, accusing me. He can be such a nervous sweaty little fellow, so pathetically anxious and afraid, he really does disappoint. I'm surprised that these timid considerations of penalty and repentance still bother him. He actually said that I should turn myself in. He said I should go to the police station the moment I get back and come clean and confess all. He's panicking. The end is drawing in, dragging itself out, and he's panicking. It's pathetic.

'If the police are waiting for me,' he said, mumbling to himself, 'I want to go quietly. I don't want any fuss.'

I ignored him. It's funny how the night can frighten.

I arrived back in London just as dawn was breaking. The time straight north and south. I abandoned the car on the Old Ford Road and walked the rest of the way home through Victoria

Park. It was a beautiful morning, a thin mist hung suspended, giving the day a mysterious sated foreboding that filled me with an excited trepidation. I sat on a bench and rolled a jazz cigarette, and then slowly took my time smoking it. I was so happy to be back. I stretched my legs out in front of me, smelt the languid morning air and felt wonderfully bodiless and intangible; it was nice. I was so relieved to be back, in spite of being wanted, and in spite of my Cinderella transformation waning. I just couldn't care – let my carriage turn back into a pumpkin, my footman back into a rat, my clothes to rags, and me into that scabrous oaf of old – that handsome but melancholy fellow – wanted in the region – he's back in town, folks, rolling home with a bad man's swagger and bloodstained cuffs!

Puff puff puff on my banger to its end – a big fat trumpet spitting blims and burning holes, all of yesterday's woes worn thin – like a dandy Yankee sitting pretty with the neighbourhood bully on his knee. My mind was rambling. The foul incoherence of existence was pressing too hard, the point of my pencil broke, and I felt him displace. There it is again, I thought – that shifty click into the abyss. It's hellish odd, and I can't explain it, but the details of doing remain…

He started scratching and rubbing the skin on my right palm, rather like Lady Macbeth. And then casting furtive paranoid glances sideways, left and right, in front and behind. And the constant call from somewhere deep within urging me to act normal… It's all so odd, but very human, the feeling of abnormality – I sometimes wonder we aren't all mutants. I suppose it might have been the jazz, but nevertheless – it unsettled. There was something shifty about the joggers, they were watching me, making me nervous and raising suspicions. I couldn't at first think why, but then I remembered that American girl with short hair and elfin looks. She went for a jog, and then she met her end. The story reported a white man sitting on a bench – sitting on this bench – a man just like me – that's why he was sweating, that's why they were looking… He stabbed her – repeatedly – at exactly this time, both arms south – and he stabbed her to death. The papers were full of it, and the television, but he was never caught. There was an appeal, and a reconstruction, posters slapped on every lamp post – they went to great lengths, local dignitaries met her parents – but nothing ever came of it, and no-one was ever caught… I sat and pondered… O pity God this miserable age.

And then I slowly began to feel a terrible creeping anxiety, a sort of horrified backward after-boding. Again it could have been the jazz but I'm not so sure – it was something other, like a weird, dread-filled post-sentiment… And then the penny dropped and like a silly parrot I realized what he was up to. He's intent on getting me caught. That's why he brought me here – that's why he sat me down and got me stoned, worked me up into a quinsy – he's out to get me captured, wants me in the bag with the sand and stones, the gutless swine. I reached for a pair of scissors to stab him, but there weren't any – so I just punched him hard on the chest, right above his heart. He felt it all right. And the bruise can prove it.

'Give yourself up,' he said, all earnest and ginger. 'Turn yourself in, man. The game's up, pal.' I hate it when he calls me pal. 'They're onto you – you can't go on like this – you can stop this – find a policeman and…'

I ignored him, got up and ambled on at a pace. The swine had tricked me – I told you you can't trust him – he's always up to something, up to no good – getting up to mischief, as Mother used to say. He walked me into that park on purpose, sat me down on that bench so that all would see – that's his game, the spineless nut, the coward frog – like a burping toad, waiting to be stabbed. That American was nothing to do with me. She's somebody else's criminal pastime, not mine... My shoulders were up, hands in pockets – legs extending, one step after another, chasing the pavement home all the way up Mare Street, Turks emerging, off at Clarence, onto Powell – only a hundred yards to go, a hundred yards from home, then fifty, twenty, nineteen, eighteen, seventeen, sixteen, fifteen...

And then I saw the blue-and-white ticker-tape strung out across the road and a policeman, standing, waiting... That gouged uncertain dread stopped in my throat... The policeman turned and looked at me. That penitent, grim, most human feeling was there again inside, churning in the gulch between right and wrong... Don't panic – stay calm – act natural – be normal. The game was up, I knew it. The swine had won. They'd found Beth and Adrian. It was all over. I could feel the guilt trickling through me, like urine down a child's leg. I walked slowly towards the policeman. He smiled.

'Good morning, sir.' He was holding a clipboard, and spoke with the mannered assurance of someone newly trained.

'Good morning,' I replied, my voice trailing and thin.

'I'm afraid there's been an incident, sir. Is there an alternative route you can take?'

'Oh...' What did he mean by 'incident'? I said nothing.

The policeman's walkie-talkie bleeped on his shoulder and made noises. He leant into it and pressed a button, but said nothing, and then returned to look at me. I spoke like a man confessing. I said: 'My name is Peter Crumb. I live at number sixty-one.'

His walkie-talkie bleeped and made a noise again. He leant into it, pressed a button on its side, and then turned away from me and said something into it, something I couldn't hear. I wiped a bead of sweat from my right eyebrow. He turned and looked at me. 'Sorry about that, sir – what did you say your name was?'

I said again: 'My name is Peter Crumb. I live at number sixty-one.'

I noticed that my finger was directionlessly pointing and ever so slightly trembling. He wrote the time down, and then my name.

'Peter Crumb, did you say? Is that with a B?'

'Yes,' I said, and then babbled on guiltily – 'I've been away – in Leeds. I've just got back. I live at number sixty-one. In the basement…'

He wrote it all down, and then tucked his pen into the neck of his bulldog clip and looked at me. He was about to speak. I felt I had to interrupt him.

'What's happened?' I enquired weakly.

'I'm afraid there's been a shooting, sir.'

A shooting? What did he mean, a shooting? I used a knife – I didn't have a gun. My forehead grizzled into wrinkled confusion.

'A stabbing?' I blurted.

'No, sir, a shooting.'

'A shooting?'

'Yes, sir.' And then he lifted the stripy ticker-tape and ushered me under. 'You can come through, sir,' he said, gesturing down the street. 'But could you try and stay on the far side of the road.'

I followed his instructions to the letter; he had, after all, been very polite. Behind me in the opposite direction, about fifty yards up the road, was a tent, I presumed covering the body. Policemen were milling and everything was cordoned off and surrounded. I couldn't believe my luck. They hadn't found Beth and Adrian – this was nothing to do with me – and the policeman hadn't recognized me – the Sudder Street scandal is obviously all but forgotten. And this was nothing to do with me, this was just some black-on-black nonsense – Operation Trident, black boy shoots black boy for mobile phone and bag of weed – case closed – done, dusted and forgotten by teatime. Jah se so.

A thin smile broke at the edges of my mouth. The police I thought – honestly, they're a fucking joke. Rudderless, clueless and utterly incompetent – is it any wonder so many law-abiding people feel nothing but utter contempt for them? Crimes go undetected, investigations get bungled – honestly, the British police are amongst the worst in the world. Rest assured, gentle reader, crime is a very low-risk activity for the criminal nowadays – the odds on getting caught are very slim, the only risk you really run is tripping a speed camera whilst making your getaway. And as for violent crime – my own particular area of expertise – well, violent crime is so rampant it's hard to comprehend – it's not a fad, it's a craze! A gathering storm, a rolling epidemic of disorder, impossible to overcome – there's just too much of it. It's curious – we consider murder and bloodshed in the twenty-first century an abomination, but we're at it more than ever. Look around you, folks – blood flows as merrily as beer on tap – that's your twenty-first century. Britain is a crime-afflicted disintegrating society, rotten to the core, wretched with scabs and festering ills and there isn't an unguent in all parliament that can bring any relief. Quite fucked, I'd say... But I digress... Yes – I do digress and may digress again. This tedious recanting of action is intolerable – this happened, that happened, he said this, I said that – to hell with it, it really is too much, what does it matter what happened? I got home, put the heating on and then made a cup of tea – there, does that make any more sense? The doing of it all, the wretched doing of it all and then thinking of it all again afterwards and writing it down, it's destroying me. Who am I writing this for? Why am I writing this – this confession?!... Because he said so, for no better reason than that. Write it down, he said – every dirty word, he said – the truth of it – the awful evil truth of it – remember? I do remember – all my grubby urges given in to. My name is Peter Crumb, soon I will be dead. That's that. Round and round it goes, ever on and on, endlessly repeated, from this day to the next – told and told again... One more day and then tomorrow... and then tomorrow.

The time is now south by south-west – morning has definitely broken. I'm locked inside my own four walls, safe and sound, sipping tea and smoking jazz. Curtains drawn... going to sleep.

## The Second Dream of Hell

I woke up. It was dark. I was lying in bed. My mother was sitting at the foot of my bed. Her back was arched and her head bent forward – staring. She was weeping pitifully, her hands held, trembling, at her mouth – the tips of her fingers resting, wet and dribbly, on her lower incisors. A catastrophe of grief, mucus, sputum and fear, smouldering into an awful twisted sorrow as she turned and looked at me, spittle trailing between her fingers and chin. I knew the truth of why – and felt afraid. It took her some time to speak, to calm herself and pronounce that awful judgement – 'I thought you were a good man, Peter… but you have made me very sad…' And then she was standing and removed, at a distance – a door behind her opened. As it did so an urgent panic broke inside me. There was only time for one last look and nine more words – 'I should not like to be in your place…' And then she was gone but her snivelling lingered… I could hear voices in the corridor, there were other people, they were about to enter, a light came on. I looked at the scab on my ankle – the flaking white skin and festering peeling scales – and I felt ashamed, a penetrating portentous shame. In a minute they'll all see it, I thought – and then I woke up… It was the feeling in the dream that made it so disturbing. It was a slow wet feeling, of permanent disgrace, about to be found out.

I am now sitting in the kitchen. I have successfully passed my toilet – Grade 5, 'soft blobs with well-defined margins'. The long arm points east, the short arm north-north-west.

All the policemen have gone and the street has reopened. The traffic flows. There are two community support officers standing at the side of the road where the tent used to be, chatting idly and joking with two traffic wardens. They are all four of them chuckling and making gestures – there's something slightly sinister about them... Probably just my paranoia... Anyway, everything is back to normal and moving slowly... He's sitting by the window, looking up into the street, like a dog waiting for a walk. I can't stop thinking about tomorrow.

Both arms up. Don's Café. Eggs over easy. Back into my routine. I have been reading an interview – a Q&A – with an actress in a magazine. A French actress. Her answers were all very ordinary and heard before – she was one of those actresses who tries to sound clever and witty. She failed. Here is my Q&A:

**When and where were you happiest?**
The winter of '96. Buddhist-baiting in Scotland.

**What is your greatest fear?**
Walking on granules of white sugar in bare feet.

**With which historical figure do you most identify?**
I'm tempted to say Job. The actress answered Joan of Arc – how
utterly preposterous!

**Which living person do you most admire?**
I find this a very difficult question to answer. Milka comes to
mind – but I don't know why.

**What is the trait you most deplore in yourself?**
Narcissistic delusions of importance.

**What is the trait you most deplore in others?**
Men are greedy fearful selfish ignorant ungrateful and cruel,
women are the same.

**What makes you depressed?**
I make me depressed.

**Where would you like to live?**
Rome.

**What is your greatest extravagance?**
Murder.

**What objects do you always carry with you?**
Various keys, lighters, cards, coins, notes, pens, pencils, a
rubber, some paper clips, a piece of string, a penknife, three
pebbles, one stone and a black rock. Does a handkerchief count
as an object?

**What do you most dislike about your appearance?**
I don't dislike my appearance at all. I'm a very handsome man,
it's often commented upon. I'm a head-turner. But if I had to
say something, then I'd say the hairs on my thighs.

**What is your most unappealing habit?**
Remembering.

**What is your favourite smell?**
Plasticine.

**What is your favourite book?**
*Where the Wild Things Are.*

**For what cause would you die?**
Cunning – the question they're really asking is, of course 'For
what cause would you kill?' My position is clear.

**Do you believe in monogamy?**
I used to, but not any more – it goes against the grain.

**What do you consider the most over-rated virtue?**
Forgiveness.

**How did you vote in the last election?**
Foolishly.

**How will you vote at the next election?**
Foolishly.

**What would your motto be?**
Keep out of reach of children.

**What lesson has life taught you?**
Never to exceed the stated dose.

**How would you like to die?**
Dramatically, with great effect.

**Do you have any regrets?**
Many. The actress said she had none, and that everything happened for a reason. What coq. The bint mistakes regret for failure and thinks failure is a bad thing.

**How would you like to be remembered?**
Fondly, with affection, but I fear I'll be remembered as evil, with revulsion and great loathing. That's if I'm remembered at all.

I hate magazines, they're such a waste of time – cheap famous faces and their measly personalities, empty sun-tanned opinions and gormless egoism. Stupid humans and their urge to be on television. I myself am an obscurist.

The headline this morning, by the way, read:

# TERROR
# ALERT

I should say so.

Left Don's and ambled on. The sun was high, the time north by north-east. The day was warming up into a real scorcher. It made no sense. The fools predict rain and wind and then we get sunshine and stillness, and an eerie ominous stillness at that. I was completely inappropriately dressed, as always – all wrapped up and crumpled in my mac and suit and tie, and sweating like a pig. Disastrous weather conditions – 'I'm sweating,' he said, and then kept repeating it, 'I'm sweating, I'm sweating... can't you feel me?'

I could feel him all right, weary and tired, unbuttoning my collar and loosening my tie.

'What are we doing?' he grumbled, whining, miffed like a child.

We were walking aimlessly and directionlessly around the Downs.

'What for?' he moaned.

'So that we don't have to think!' I snapped, scolding him with an exasperated fervour. The heat was getting to me, people were looking. One day it's raining, the next day it's blistering sunshine. The flowers must be so confused, not to mention the trees. It's ridiculous, we can no longer even depend on the seasons for any sort of continuity – what must the birds make of it? All is at sea and hopelessly at odds, mutiny from stern to bow. I ground my teeth and said, 'Yes.' He agreed and we both fell silent...

We ambled on for a length or so and then stopped and sat down on a bench. The silence between us was strong, both of us knew exactly what the other was thinking but neither of us was going to say anything. We were each waiting for the other to speak first. Inevitably it fell to me to break the silence. It always falls to me. I took a deep breath, in through my mouth and out through my nose. He hates it when I breathe backwards.

'Today is your last day,' I solemnly began. There was a pause.

'Yes,' he said, cheerlessly matter-of-fact.

'We should do something special.'

'Yes,' again without enthusiasm. And then he sighed and rolled his feet onto their sides, inverting them beneath his ankles and turning the soles of his shoes in on themselves. It was such a defeated action, a little action, but one that seemed to reverberate through him and change his whole demeanour. He suddenly seemed utterly crushed and beaten, totally deflated. It was almost as if he had shrunk. He just sat there, staring silently at the shadow in the space between his feet. A lonely, broken man, lost in quiet contemplation, his end now only a day away. I closed my eyes and placed my hand on my chest and felt my heart beating. There you are, I thought, and may have muttered it. My hand was pressed flat around my left nipple, it was hot and wet with sweat, I felt a certain sensual delight touching myself in this way – feeling for that distant buried pulse... There you are, I thought, there you are – that calm, slow, easy beat, repeating, as little drops of sweat slip and course and join and go. It made me think of Father and the word 'worry'... I remember I could feel the faintest wisps of a breeze too, gently tickling the hairs on the back of my hand, which I held perfectly still and stared at for some time. I also noted that the skin at the edges of my fingernails is flaking and torn, and stained a dirty nicotine umber. It reminded me of my uncle Eric. His fingers were marked with this same orange discoloration. I let the memory settle, looked away and ran three fingers backwards through my jumbled strands of thinning hair. The sun was on my limbs, sucking and softening. A day so out of sorts, and far too hot. A bright red burning day, completely at odds with the season. And people everywhere. As soon as the sun comes out they all come out, exposing themselves and oiling themselves. Awkward corpulent lumps of pink jellied flesh, bleached white on the yellow grass, tanning green... The vanity of these ruthless humans...

I glanced at my watch – the long arm was north, the short arm north-north-east. Half the day gone and still nothing done. He cracked his jaw, got up and without saying anything wandered on. I followed him, looking, seeing and thinking, a slow soggy shuffle through the sunshine. We hadn't gone ten paces before he started yanking at my tie, hurriedly undoing it, jerking my neck and pulling it from around me. He held it for a time in his left hand, trailing it along the ground beside me like a recalcitrant schoolboy chivying home, and then he let it go. It dropped from his fingers and spooled into little ox-bow folds on the path. He didn't look back or pick it up, he just left it... Then he reached into the pockets of my mac and removed my keys and Beth and Adrian's keys and my tobacco and a lighter, and stuffed them all into my trouser pockets, which were already heavily weighted with Her Majesty's shrapnel. Then he went through all the pockets of my suit jacket, removing my wallet, which he stuffed into my back trouser pocket, and my handkerchief, which he stuffed in with the keys. My pockets were bulging – I know it looks unsightly and ruins the line of your trousers, but, as I think I've already mentioned, I'm a pocket-bulger by nature. He peeled the mac and suit jacket from my back, roughly bundled them together over my arm, crossed to a waste basket – teeming with filth and little bags of dog shit – and dumped them both in. The relief from the heat was immediate. I was aware that people were watching me but they didn't seem particularly concerned or interested, he certainly paid them no mind, just untucked my shirt and gave it a good billowing. A delicious gulp of crisp coolness splashed the sweat from my chest and peeled cold between my shoulders. He let out a deep sigh, undid the top three buttons of my shirt and rolled my sleeves up... Bizarre, I thought, and it isn't even April... The sky was so blue, a vivid luminous blue, not a cloud in sight. Most odd. An aeroplane banked high into the sun. I shaded my eyes. The planet is dying, he sighed, but it does it so, so beautifully...

We ambled on, off the Downs and onto Queensdown Road, then Clarence Road and then down towards Mare Street. It's my usual route, familiar and often walked, I like it for that reason. He was gambolling on ahead of me, as is his wont, he always walks too quickly, it's as if he's ashamed of me and doesn't want to be seen with me, doesn't want people to know that we're together – which is ridiculous, as it's as plain as day, for all to see, that we are naturally each other's. We go together like mango and prawns. At the Narrow Way there was suddenly an overwhelming glut of people, an all-sorts collection of hideous mutations – every shape and size, colour and creed. Human doings and their insatiable appetites, ravenously

shopping. He was loving it, and straight in amongst them –
moving fast, freer than before – weaving in and out between
them – enjoying himself, I thought. Look at him, atwixt them,
with his shirt sleeves rolled, lengthening his gait, on a
summer's day in spring – lost among the infinite variety –
legion between them, all God's children and there he is – look
at him, enjoying himself…

It put me in mind of a very vivid memory I have of being
allowed, as a child, to go to the shops to buy some sweets by
myself for the first time. I can't have been much older than five
– the same age as Emma. You see, it was the urge to repeat –
that instinctive human urge to repeat, copy, pass on and do
again. I remember feeling so happy at being allowed to go by
myself, and I was up for the assignment – I showed no fear,
none at all – I confidently marched off down that enormous
hill, shirt sleeves rolled, lengthening my gait – I knew that
Mother was watching, but I didn't look back. I patiently waited
at the side of the road, remembered to look left and right, the
red car stopped, and then I crossed the zebra's back and
skipped into the shop. I bought a Sherbet Dib-Dab, some milk
teeth and a Curly Wurly, and I gobbled the lot on the way back.
I was so happy. Everything was full of colour. I burst in
through the back door, smiling a big black sticky-fingered
liquorice smile. I remember Mother wiped my mouth with a
yellow J-cloth – and I remember feeling her pride as she wres-
tled with me next to her. I can remember it all so clearly. I can
smell it… Emma's first solo venture to the shops wasn't quite
as successful. I remember reassuring Valerie that she'd be fine,
that everything would be all right. But she wasn't fine, and

everything wasn't all right. I watched her walk away, she looked back at me and waved – her little hand with all five fingers splayed. It's in an instant that everything goes wrong. It's all of a sudden – and then there's nothing anyone can do… She made it to the shop all right – the shopkeeper remembered her. She was an Asian woman, just like the other one, she remembered Emma, she said she bought a Strawberry Mivvi – they found it on the pavement. I wanted her to feel my pride. I wanted to tickle her, and squeeze her and make her giggle – I wanted to wipe her mouth with a clean yellow J-cloth. I wanted to hold her, safely, and know that she was loved. I wanted it all not to be true, and for the horror to end. But I digress…

He was swinging his arms with his shirt sleeves rolled, lengthening his gait and bowling into Marks & Sparks. What's he up to? I thought, and followed him through the store towards the menswear department, and then watched from a distance as he bought two leather belts – one black and one brown, both made in England of genuine leather.

'What are they for?' I asked as we made our way out.

'What do you think they're for?' he tersely replied.

He didn't have to say any more. I knew, and thought about tomorrow.

I remember at this juncture, just as we were setting off down Mare Street, I remember acknowledging two things. The first was just how stoned I felt – all dem damn bangers piling up, I thought. The second was that I was being watched by a black man. He seemed vaguely familiar, but I couldn't think from where. A long thin dreadlocked Rastaman, with his eyes on me – watching me. I remember thinking, distinctly remember thinking, what's he looking at? Looking at me like that for? I know I'm a head-turner – but this was something else. Yes, I remember thinking that – and carried on thinking it, and going over it, and wondering about it, and worrying about it, and not paying attention to where we were heading, until all of a sudden – I looked up and… Oh my God… My spine straightened and a cold twitch pinched the back of my neck… Sudder Street… I was standing outside the newsagent's. Its windows had been shuttered and boarded up, that familiar blue-and-white ticker-tape was strung, knotted and twisted, through a grille in front of the door. People were passing, watching me. I could tell they had suspicions. I felt his breath beneath my nostrils and self-consciously looked away, back at the scrawled and papered hoardings behind me.

'Do you remember how spotty her chin was?' he said, rounding on me.

I didn't reply.

'We should have had those Double Deckers.'

I didn't know what he was talking about.

'Do you remember how she was shaking?'

I couldn't listen to him. I jerked my head violently away from him, trying to escape him.

'Shit in your pants and that's how they'll find you! Remember that? The fear in her eyes. You said you could smell her – then – wallop! Remember? The smell of her fear!'

I knew what he was doing – he was trying to razz me – always, all of them – razzing me, sneering, jeering at me – forcing me out into the open –

'I can smell it on you!' I suddenly blurted, barking madly and wildly reeling. It was a mistake. A young man walking past me stopped and turned and looked at me. He looked aggrieved. His face contorted into an offended sneer. 'Can smell what on me?' he demanded indignantly. A cold wave of troubled confusion washed through me. He was a big lad in a white tracksuit, with a fashionable haircut and gold jewellery. I could tell he had working-class morals. I thought he was going to hit me. The craven beetle in my shoes shuffled and muttered in flustered supplicating embarrassment – 'Sorry, I was, nothing, I'm sorry – I'm...'

The fella tutted, muttered 'fucking twat' – loud enough for all to hear – and then walked on, shaking his head, happy to conclude I was nothing more than mental. I felt ashamed and frightened. I put my eyes to the floor and noted that my heart was beating and that the skin between my eyes was twitching ... He didn't say anything, he didn't have to, I knew what he was thinking. He's doing everything he can to catch me, I thought. He's chasing me down, running me to ground and barking all the way home. Never return to the scene of the crime – never, ever, never. A foolish thing to do... I ground my teeth and said 'Yes.' He agreed. We ambled home in silence, a bitter taste in my mouth and an air between us.

The house was quiet when we got in. I knew what he was thinking, so it came as no surprise when he suggested we have a look in on Beth and Adrian.

But I shouldn't have listened – it was a mistake.

'Get the keys,' he ordered, 'and stop sweating.'

What did I expect to find? I closed their front door quietly behind me and carefully made my way down the corridor towards the living room. I stopped in the doorway and looked at Adrian. The air smelt a little sour, putrefaction was setting in. I followed the dried black blood trail through to the bedroom doorway and looked in on Beth. Those pretty hazel eyes of hers had soured into cloudy regret, a mournful dead lament … Another two dead, I thought, and slowly decomposing. Another two forgotten, and left to rot. And nobody knows, nobody knows but me…

As I was leaving I noticed that a light on their answering machine was blinking. I pressed a button and the electronic voice of a very posh woman announced, 'You have one new message.' She stressed the word 'one'. There was a bleep and then the message played. It was from a bloke called Johnnie, just phoning to see what they were up to. He said he hadn't spoken to either of them in ages but that it was nothing important. He just wanted to see if they fancied meeting up some time and hoped they were well. He said he had a new mobile number which he repeated twice. I wrote it down on the back of a menu from a local curry house. Johnnie sounded very nervous, and spoke with a desperate cheeriness. He sounded guilty and alone. It made me think of me. I used to sound like that, I thought – I used to make phone calls like that. I tucked the menu with his number into my back pocket and thought, maybe I'll phone you, Johnnie, maybe I'll phone and say hello.

I glanced around and noticed both their mobiles plugged into a socket, charging. I turned them both on and checked their messages. Adrian didn't have any – it surprised me, you'd have thought that at the very least his work would have phoned, but no. Who knows what his work was – maybe he didn't work with others, maybe he worked alone. Beth had one message, from a girl called Maria, saying she was back (she didn't say from where) and to give her a call. It saddened me, this lack of interest in their lives. I thought these people were the connected type. Now I think they were the lonely type, the type that only had each other. I locked their front door behind me, went downstairs, let myself into my flat, sat down and felt very depressed. A deep sadness welled up in me, and a swollen lump of emotion stuck in my throat, choking me. I didn't cry, but I did brood. There they all are, dead and rotting and forgotten. Decomposing by the day and nobody knows, only I know… I made a cup of tea, and wrote it all down.

The time is now south by south-south-east. I've had a bath and calmed down, put on some clean clothes, freshened up and am heading out. It's a beautiful evening, my last, and I'm going to make the most of it.

There has been an extraordinary turn of events. I have been on the television again. I am on the television now. I am watching myself, and the nation watches with me. I shall explain.

The time was straight north and south when I left the flat. I hopped onto the 38 bus at Clapton Pond and nestled into my second favourite seat, right at the front of the top deck. My favourite seat, at the back of the top deck, had already been taken by a disgustingly fat Afro-Caribbean woman with an enormous backside spread out over two seats. Will she have to pay twice, I thought? No, of course she won't – some poor bugger will have to stand downstairs or wait at the bus stop for another bus because her arse is the size of a buffalo's. Such people make me sick. She sat there hunched over her McDonald's chicken dippers, shovelling them into her craving insatiable gullet. The bus stank of processed glutamates. It was intolerable. I gave her a contemptuous look and pointedly opened all the windows, not that she noticed – she seemed oblivious to any offence the sight and stink of her might be causing. Typical lard-arsed human, I thought, selfishly unaware of anything other than her own voracious appetites, stuck in a bell jar of gluttony – guzzling and burping, swilling down a bucketful of fizzy pop and then panting with an exhausted fervour and starting to sweat. It filled me with rage – the fat ones are the worst. Honestly – I'm sure you agree – people that fat shouldn't be allowed, they're freaks. They drain resources and are always whingeing – they blame their glands or plead obesity, but the truth is they're greedy and lazy and indulgent – they are the apotheosis of decadent Western culture, and if I had things my way I'd herd them all, like cattle, into the most desperate quarter of starving Africa and then leave them there to rot. Starve them all to death. And I'd broadcast it live on national television every night. A sort of *Big Brother* peepshow festival of fat. *Fat in the Heart of Africa*, I'd call it, and I'd get Bob Geldof to present it – Bob and his spaniel sidekick Boner... Yes – but I digress, forgive me, I'm ranting – I'm a little over-excited – manic even. The end is very near and, as I've said, there has been an extraordinary turn of events...

To resume – the bus made off on its rounds and quickly filled. Next to me sat a very polite, if not a little prim, white girl. She was very English-looking, about twenty-eight and dressed in a pair of simple plimsolls, a long orange cotton skirt that I would describe as hippyish, a plain white t-shirt and a hijab. Yes – that's right – a hijab. A rather beautiful light-blue hijab that framed her porcelain-white English features. A convert, I thought, and nervously recalled the headline – Terror Alert. I glanced backwards over my shoulder around the bus – nine-tenths of the skin on the top deck was dark, a third of it in the hijab and three-eighths of it wearing a beard. I looked back at the girl next to me, she was very attractive – in a Western way – that is to say, skinny, white and well proportioned, with long legs and a cute arse – good to fuck, porno style. I let my look linger on her, linger long enough for her to know that I was looking at her, but she didn't look back. It doesn't do for a Muslim woman to look at a man, it can lead to all sorts. I momentarily pictured her spread out naked in front of me, with her legs apart and her cunt glistening. She's not an extremist, I thought. Just a silly middle-class girl, lost for a time in her twenties, posing devotion to Allah. Whatever gets you through the night. Her mother and father must be very disappointed. Christmas will never be the same…

She crossed her legs away from me and got out a book – *Harry Potter and the Goblin's Cock*, or something like that. I settled back into my seat, looked out of the window and quietly contemplated the evening ahead. It was a beautiful evening, an Indian evening – the clouds rippling long and thin through a magnificent crimson sky. And beneath, a heaving multitude of lurching humans, spilling into the streets, out of pubs and bars and restaurants and cafés, drinking and laughing and chattering. Drunken drivellings, the lot of them – enjoying themselves, promoting themselves, and posturing. Look at them, I thought, all of these people – just as many, and as many more – all full of hopes and dreams – all of them deluded. Searching for something better – contentment, love, success. Someone to fuck. Or someone to blame. Or just a little chip of something extra, a moment's brief respite from the nasty brutish solitary and cruel lot that is theirs. Poor awful humans, stupid to the end – waiting and hoping, enduring and surviving their meagre lives, certain of nothing but the sanctity of their own existence. All the same and one, but separate and alone… I sighed and closed my eyes, not knowing where to look, where I was heading or what I was going to do when I got there. It was my last night, and I was determined to make the most of it. The bus rumbled on, panting its way into town, I jostled off into a gentle doze…

When I woke the bus was shuddering, wheezing and coughing its way into Victoria Station. It pulled up second in a shattered line of resting 38s. The lights went off and on and off again, and the remaining stragglers got up and shuffled off. I remained seated, not going anywhere. My trousers were wet with semen. I glanced out of the window and saw the white Muslim girl, about whom I had been dreaming, disappearing into the station. I touched the wet patch on my trousers and felt the tip of my dwindling erection beneath. I wonder if she knew, I thought – and hoped that she had. I haven't had a wet dream in years. A wet dream is the most heavenly experience in the entire lexicon of human experiences...

I dreamt that she turned to face me, met my eyes, and looked at me. I dreamt that in front of everyone on the bus lifted her t-shirt to reveal her white naked skin and her large swollen breasts. My lips were on her, licking and nibbling her nipples. Her body was taut and arched and writhing, her head thrown back. She stood up and pulled her skirt up around her waist and then pushed her naked bristling pubes forward into my face. The smell of her was intoxicating, a musty dampness. I brought my mouth close into her sex and tasted her, she was sweet, like tangerines, and starting to moan. I cupped her buttocks in my hands and rolled and kneaded her flesh, my tongue tasting its way towards her clitoris and then working it with short sharp cat-like licks. I could feel her reaching and undoing my flies and fondling my cock – I was more than fully engorged. She knelt down in front of me, opened her mouth and showed me her tongue – it was a dark purple, matching exactly the colour of my knob. She wrapped her lips around the end of me and slurped and sucked and gurgled. I was going to come. She grabbed my balls and squeezed hard, pinching the base of my cock between her thumb and forefinger to stop me – this girl knew what she was doing. She then got down on all fours in the aisle between the seats, put her hands on her arse and peeled her thighs apart. Her pussy was clean and pink and wet. Her eyes were on me, over her shoulder, beckoning me to fuck her. The bus pulled up at a stop. I knelt down behind her and entered her. People got on and off, took their seats and watched as I fucked her. She was working her pussy muscles, gripping and rippling the length of my cock as I violently jammed away at her... It didn't take long. As I came I pushed my thumb into her anus and she barked *Allahu akbar*, like a dog. I think I moaned. She must have known. I remember grunting and jerking and then her skin suddenly turned an electric copper green. And then she looked at me – met my eyes and looked into me. It was that rat from Sudder Street. Her chin bleeding puss. I pulled myself out of her, revolted. She scuttled across the floor and disappeared up a drainpipe. She's a haunter, that one. And then I woke. My trousers wet with semen. I glanced back out of the window. The girl had gone. There were people everywhere, moving in every direction. The bus in front was packed to the gunnels and slowly starting to pull out... And then it happened.

A sudden bright white flash exploded before me. A kaleidoscope of silver lines drawn in rapid succession carnivalled in a blizzard of raging energy. A roaring booming explosion chased a hideous clattering screaming growl, and then a tearing rip of thunderous destruction as metal and glass ruptured and shattered in every direction. A hot black cloud of burning smoke and the unmistakable stench of sulphur engulfing everything in a raging pall of silence and then, in an instant, bursting open

210

again into a hideous howling cacophony of screaming terror. The mutilated slaughtered cries of the damned. I touched my face and felt that one side had been lacerated with tiny cuts and was wet with blood. My eyes were stinging and blurred. In my ears there was a terrifying high-pitched whine, everything was abstracted and vivid. The back of the bus in front had been totally blown away, sheaves of twisted mangled metal had been thrown out, ripped and gnarled and torn apart, screaming jagged edges twisted black with fire and blood. The horror of bodies thrown in every direction, ripped and split apart. The dismembered remains strewn in a ten-metre radius. And the screaming, the screaming cries for help – Help me! – Help me! – Please somebody – help me!... I sat and watched. My clothes had been ripped from my body, my chest was bare and covered in dark soot and sweat and thin tracks of blood. I didn't feel anything. Any pain. My head was still ringing from the explosion, my senses acutely aware but blinkered and jumping from one individual piece of information to the next, but doing so with incredible speed and rapidity, which made everything seem slow. I stood up, and acknowledged the fact that I was standing. I turned and slowly made my way down from the top deck, emerging at the back of the bus. People were running away, others, at a safe distance, were standing and watching... I turned, and without thinking walked directly towards the exploded bus. I stopped and looked at it. It was an incredible sight – an hallucination almost, distorted and dreamlike in the shimmering heat. The entire rear section had been blown apart and torn open. The front of the bus I had been sitting in was no more than three metres away and had taken its fair share of the blast. I looked back up at where I had been sitting. All the windows had been blown out and a section of the front corner of the roof had been peeled back. It was a miracle that I had survived. I put my eyes to the ground. Between the two buses lay bloody burning carnage. The walking wounded were starting to emerge, their bodies exposed, some more than others, men and women, ripped and blackened, staggering, bewildered and confused, half dead, about to die, wishing they were dead or wondering why they weren't. We all looked at each other, and then looked away. One man was naked, his back was on fire, all his skin had blistered. He fell to his knees and burnt. A woman, with a long length of serrated metal ripped through her abdomen, writhed and spasmed in agony. A man tried to stand but only had one leg and fell awkwardly, slipping in his own blood. Another simply stood and wept. There were sirens and screams. People calling. Lacerated flesh. General chaos and confusion. Everything was cloaked in an evil darkness and choked with foul stinking fumes. I stood alone and stared. Surely this was Hell. The torn severed remains of what must have been a young girl lay folded and chopped at my feet, her left arm and half her torso. Her breast was young, the areola pink. On her wrist she wore a watch, a simple watch with a red leather strap and an old-fashioned round face. The short arm pointed south, the long arm south-south-east... I moved towards the bus, closer and closer to the epicentre of the blast, drawn to the destruction like a thief towards his booty. I clambered in. The horror was unimaginable and indescribable. The awful stink of petrol and rubber and plastic and blood and metal and sulphur. Strange noises, straining and tearing, cracking violently in the blackest and inkiest darkness. A woman still sitting in her seat, her hand still gripping her bag, a foot in her lap and her head blown clean off her shoulders. Beyond her, a shallow pool of blood and intestines were boiling, actually boiling. Another, I think it was a woman although there was no way of telling, lay screwed up in a corner, her limbs wrapped around her in a violent derangement and her body horribly twisted, snarled, crushed and tangled, with large chunks of flesh ripped out of her like massive bite marks... And then I saw something move. I turned and stooped and peered through the smoke. A little girl, no older than Emma. She was screaming, trapped beneath an entangled web of twisted metal and burning plastic. She was calling to me to help her. I didn't think – I just moved towards her and grabbed her and pulled her, violently wrenching her free from the mangled scrap. I pulled her close into my arms and held her, safe and protected. She was tiny. I clambered back out of the bus, ambulances were arriving and the police were now everywhere. I made my way quickly back towards the retreating cordon of people. All of them were watching me – every eye in the crowd was on me, gawping at me – horrified, and amazed – their cameras and camcorders and mobile phones all aimed at me, filming me, as I made my way out of the growling burning wreck, a little girl held close and safe in my arms, both of us, still, miraculously, alive.

And now they can't stop showing it – over and over they keep on playing it. It's good footage. Natasha Kaplinsky called me The Hero of Bus 38. Alastair Stewart repeated it and then so did Katie Derham. They all want to know who the hero of bus 38 is. After my amateur heroics I didn't stick around to sign any autographs, I just left the girl with a medic, took a blanket and disappeared into the crowd. I quietly shuffled off without giving any interviews.

And it was a hellishly long plod home, I can tell you. All the way from Victoria to Hackney – it's a bloody long way. Wrapped in a blanket, bleeding and aching, only hours left to live, one step in front of the other, nothing to do but reflect... and plod on, and plod on, slowly, backwards over it all, forward to the end... I got in, made a cup of the Earl and collapsed with a jazz in front of the telly.

Every channel is giddy with it – continual terror updates, eye witness reports, live footage, breaking news – they can't contain themselves. There have been four bombs in all, this time all on buses. The classic burning cross spread out over London once again. Euston, Victoria, Ladbroke Grove and Old Street. From the north to the south, the east to the west, the Father, Son and Holy Ghost. Amen. *Allahu akbar*. The death toll stands at twenty-eight. Many more wounded... And there I am again – they just can't stop playing it – it is good footage, clear, in focus, broadcast-quality stuff, caught from every angle – me entering the burning bus, bloody and bare-chested like Rambo, and then emerging moments later with a little girl held close and safe in my arms. The life-saving heroics of the insanely brave – and nobody knows who he is – The Hero of Bus 38. Or the guilty man that God forgot.

The time is east... The end is nigh.

# SUNDAY

Perhaps I shouldn't have listened – certainly not obeyed. But that's all with hindsight and easy to say now. I'm yielding by nature and giving in is easy. I'm not looking for forgiveness or trying to make excuses, but when I think of how it all began and where we are now – and all that's gone on in between… Well, yes, I have to concede, a man of evil conscience cannot act well, and taking up my pen was a very naughty and very silly thing to do. Yes, that was my first sin… But what of it, so long as the sun goes on setting and so long as there's someone around to take its picture, well, we can all live happily with that… But I digress, deviating from my course yet again – oh yes, I'm a deviant all right, meandering away from my plan, my grand idea. I must stay on track and see it through, stop this skirting and get on with it – time is short and I'm dodging, I must get on and complete. These last few jumbled recollections will have to suffice and conclude. I've tried to be honest and plain, I've done my best, but what remains, scribbled here, is really nothing very much at all, there is immeasurably more inside. I shall rewind, and for one last time recall. A little jazz to help me on my way…

His first words to me this morning, before I'd even opened my eyes, were: 'Today, I am going to kill you.'

And he wasn't joking – and now there's no avoiding it – the outcome, that is, not the action. But I'm getting ahead of myself and you'll hardly understand… The morning's rituals unfolded routinely. I woke, as usual, in a shocking condition – something approaching a jittering gimp. My body black and broken, filthy with sweat and as stiff as sugared toffee. My limbs weary and aching, my skin creeping and my mind clattering with jumbled, frenzied thoughts, all of them feverishly at odds. I sat up and shook myself and shivered, and then pulled and stretched myself into some sort of working order, and then hobbled awkwardly over to the mirror and, bleary-eyed, peered in. What a pained disfigured wretch appeared – still guilty and afraid, but now more so, and worse… My face and shoulders lacerated with a thousand tiny cuts – like some garish tribal tattoo, marking my disgrace – a dark dense multitude of little lines exploding outwards over my features, incised into my skin. Horrible and beautiful… I admired myself and then felt mournful, looked at the floor, and thought of breakfast.

'It's just a day like any other,' he muttered, rasping, as we eased our way awkwardly down the corridor and into the kitchen. I made some toast and tea, and then sat down and sipped and chewed and forced myself to swallow until I'd had my fill… And then I remember he momentarily left me, and went and sat by himself on the green chair by the door and did one of his drawings. A self-portrait. I remember the shadows at the edges, and in between objects and in corners, held my attention, misty and obscure – and I remember an emptiness filled me, and the muted unprepossessing dullness of nothing pushed darkly inward. It was a sort of freedom... But it didn't last long.

The television burbled, zealously regurgitating yesterday's terror.

'This story'll play for weeks,' he said. 'They'll milk it for all it's worth – nothing else'll have a look-in now. You'd have to rape the Queen to break these headlines. Your antics are small fry compared to this. You might as well not have bothered.'

I ignored him. He's going to be at me all day, I thought.

'Yes,' he said, barking at the wall, 'I am.' His tone was adamant.

The death toll has risen to 102.

'By the end of today that'll be at least 103,' he sneered and then facetiously added, 'Maybe that'll be tomorrow's headline – Hero of Bus 38 Found Dead in Basement Flat.' And then he sniggered like a dirty baboon – tormenting me, even at this late stage, his nostrils flaring and his hairs vibrating... I remember there was something about the sight of him in that moment that really sickened me, and I remember he felt it in my expression, and I remember thinking: I did that... It was a very strange and uncomfortable moment. Neither of us knew where to look. I remember taking note of it and thinking I must write this down – it seemed like a very big and important thing at the time – righteous even. But now, having written it down, it just seems silly and vapid and nothing very much at all… Anyway, he lit a cigarette and watched it burn. The little girl I saved has been scrubbed and polished and reunited with her father. Her name is Sienna. The right side of her face is tattooed with the same dark scratchings as mine. We are of the same tribe. Katie Razzall from Channel 4 news asked her if she had a message for the man that saved her. She said she wanted to say thank you and hoped I would come and have tea with them at their house soon. He said we should have kept her. I ignored him, and turned the television off. We sat for a moment in silence, listening to the hush fizzle through the room and then slowly ebb away into quiet. And then he got up and looked at me.

'Come on,' he said. 'Let's crumble on…'

I followed him into the kitchen and watched as he put the butter and the marmalade and the milk back into the fridge and then put the sugar back on the shelf. His actions were mechanical and unthinking. He emptied the half-chewed remains of my breakfast into the bin and then washed and rinsed my cup and plate, my knife and spoon, and dried them all and put them away. Then he wet a cloth and wiped the surfaces, gathering crumbs into his left palm. He rinsed his hands beneath the tap and then rinsed the cloth, tightly squeezing and re-squeezing it, enjoying its wetness and dribbling cold sogginess. Then he folded the cloth into a neat rectangle and draped it daintily over the tap. Then he dried his hands on the tea towel and then folded that into a neat rectangle and draped it over the oven. Then he looked at everything, and remembered it all… the stained grey sink and drainer, those broken tiles, that large pot of oversized utensils too big for the drawer, the small pot of wooden spoons – characterfully stained a rich reddy brown – the salt and pepper – oily and clogged – that crack in the surface full of filth impossible to remove, a bottle of Tesco's Finest olive oil, aspirant, new and unopened. That odd collection of jugs bought in market towns on weekends away, never to be used. My old Baby Belling. The toaster and kettle – a set from the Hannai lifestyle range from Woolworths. My fridge. The bin, and the table I painted green to match the chair by the door beneath the light switch, too often fingered, and that bowl full of things and bits, and the clock, and that postcard of the Marx brothers prancing. He looked at it all. And remembered it all. And then he shuffled out, and into the front room…

Last night's blanket was thrown over the sofa, he crossed and folded it into a neat rectangle and then draped it over the arm, then he plumped the cushions and arranged them, lolloping comfortably into one another. There was something sad and pathetic about the sight of those cushions – they reminded me of me and him, drunk on a bench after one too many black-and-tans, nestling heads and burping… He picked my shoes and socks up, tucked my socks into my shoes and then placed them, tidily out of the way, on the small wooden chair by the window. My fingers came to rest on the back of the chair, and I remember it felt warm. I squeezed it and felt its hardness and woodenness, I stroked it, trailing my fingers affectionately, and then he pulled my hand away – jerking it, ouch-like, back into his body. It was a strange action, full of fear, and it confused me, distracting me… And then the next thing I remember he was staring at the telephone… And it was troubling him… He stared at it for some time, trying to decide something – whether he should or whether he shouldn't… I remember I waited, and felt very anxious… And then he shuffled tentatively towards the telephone, hesitantly lifted the receiver, and nervously listened to the dialling tone. He reached into my back pocket and removed a flyer for a local curry house, he placed it by the telephone and dialled the mobile phone number scrawled across the back of it.

'Hello?' said Johnnie. The reception wavered… 'Hello?'

'Hello…' The connection settled. 'My name's Peter, erm…' His voice trailed, whispering thinly. 'I'm a friend of Beth and Adrian's.'

'Oh, right,' said Johnnie, cheerily.

'Yees…' said Peter, not so. 'You left a message on their answering machine… erm, I hope you don't mind me calling.'

'No, not at all.'

'No… You said in your message you hadn't seen Beth and Adrian in some time.'

'No – that's right I've –'

'Yes,' he said interrupting, and then he paused… and Johnnie listened, his qualms ripening.

'Has something happened?'

'I'm afraid… Beth and Adrian were involved in an incident, and I'm afraid… they are no longer with us.'

'What?'

'I'm sorry to say, Beth and Adrian are dead.'

There was a pause.

'I'm afraid…' The reception wavered again, a lost hissing crackled and fizzed and then found itself and settled. I let the moment roll, his angst gathering momentum.

'I'm afraid…' He closed his eyes, and let go – 'I stabbed them.'

A cold rush tingled through me. It was quite exquisite.

'What?' stammered Johnnie.

And then out it all poured – the maniacal, incoherent, drivelling ravings of an evil preening madman.

'I stabbed them. I slit his throat… and gutted her… I killed them. I killed them both – I stabbed him… stabbed her… I did it… He was watching me. Persistently watching me – I told him, I said to him – in my own back garden – but no, it was intolerable – I was trying to be polite – I offered him a scone – I was on the television – and they weren't the only ones – I'm known throughout the region – there were others too – just put out for the bin men – Two Found Dead in E8 Bloodbath – Woman's Body Found in Bin Bag.'

I listened to myself, and for the first time in a long time, heard myself.

'Who is this?' Johnnie protested, indignant, his shock galvanized into outrage.

'My name is Peter Crumb!' he snarled viciously, his tone emphatic and absolute. 'I am the guilty man that God forgot. I am the hero of bus 38. I am the man that lives beneath, my name is Peter Crumb.' And then he slammed the receiver down hard against the handset and ripped the cable from the wall. It was all quite bizarre. He was sobbing and shaking – full of sorrow and despair – on his knees, holding himself, terrified, waiting for something to happen, his teeth exposed, his incisors grinding, sweat pooling and his lips twitching. And then he suddenly flinched and turned and looked at me – held my eyes and looked into me. I saw a terrible pitiful fear, and then he looked away, ashamed. His fingers knuckled and twisted, his back stooped with his head crooked upwards at the ceiling, listening to Beth and Adrian's telephone ringing... It rang fifteen times and then fell silent. I didn't move... 'That'll be Johnnie,' he said, 'checking to see that they're all right. Now that he's had no reply he'll call the police, and he'll tell them.' What will he tell them? I thought. He'll tell them he's just had a phone call from a madman called Peter Crumb claiming to be the hero of bus 38 who ranted nonsense about scones and stabbings. The police will think he's mad and hang up. That's if he even gets through – he'll be directed to an answering machine – press one for a mugging, two for a stabbing, three for some hairy, four for a murder and five to return to the menu. The police are far too busy chasing terror to look into this nonsense, it'll be weeks or months before they get around to crank calls – at the very most they'll send a community support officer over to have a look-in. The community support officer will ring the buzzer and get no reply. Then they'll file a report, probably in appalling English, saying that they rang the buzzer and got no reply, and then that'll be that.

He turned and brusquely crossed to the door, grabbed the door handle and held it – cold in my hand, the brass roundness of it flat against my palm. And then he suddenly pulled the door open towards me, a rush of displaced air billowed all around me... It was nice... He did it again, and then again, and again and again – with increasing wildness and fervour, over and over, pitching and swinging the door – slamming it back and forth, open and closed, until his arms grew weary and his panting strained... As I said, it was all very odd... We took a moment to recover and then puttered up the corridor. An assorted row of socks were laid out to dry along the length of the radiator, all of them stepping west, never to be worn again. He picked them off randomly, two at a time, and rolled them into little balls – six odd pairs in all. He stared at them and squeezed them, fondled them, felt their softness, and held them, then brought them up to his nostrils and smelt them, inhaling deeply – in through his nose and out through his mouth, the right way round... He thought of Milka and her bottom in blue velour sweatpants, and the kind words she had spoken. He remembered her touch and her gentle tones, and her Eastern inflections, dancing lightly, a bright white chimera with golden blonde locks, crackling static. She'll be the one that finds you, he said – she'll be the one they talk to – she'll say kind things, and remember gentle truths. Come on, he said – don't worry, it's all going to be all right – come on, he said, let's have a look in here. We stepped into the spare room, its emptiness immediately overwhelming. That stain on the carpet watching as we crossed to the window and looked out into the garden. Today will be a beautiful day, he said – everything in it will shine and be wonderful – nothing will break it, and nothing be wrong with it. A beautiful new day – complete and full and perfect. And then he placed his hand on the window pane and splayed his fingers and pressed gently against the glass – reaching out to feel the cold bright splendour of the day beyond. It was there for a moment, simple, beautiful and true, and then it was gone. I closed my eyes and rested my forehead against the frame. I could feel his breath close and damp against the cold glass.

I opened my eyes and watched as the pane clouded over into a large white circle of breathy haze. He drew a face – two dots for eyes, a curving line, bent at the edges, for a mouth. The expression artistically miserable. The mist receded and the face disappeared, leaving nothing but two greasy finger prints and an oily smear, signing off. He turned and shuffled back out into the corridor and then into the bedroom. I sat on the edge of the bed and then lay down. I closed my eyes and tried to remember, tried to remember something about her, something that I had forgotten, but I couldn't... There is nothing left now. It is all forgotten, what little there was, it has all gone. Emma and Valerie... and whoever I was... In the end, it is all just forgotten.

I must have sat up, and then got up, I probably sat up and then got up – or remained seated, yes, probably remained seated and staring – if not for a bit then for a long time – I can't remember. He rolled a jazz and we smoked it... yes... and then we wandered back into the front room and sat down on the sofa. He turned the television on, flicked through half a dozen channels and then turned it off again. Yes, that was pretty much it – that was pretty much the total of it. I'm sure there were other things too, probably big things that I'm forgetting, important things, important thoughts about the meaning of it all, things I ought to remember but can't – things I should have noticed but didn't. I remember I stared at a bit of old Rizla paper, flittering on the floor in a draught by the front door. I remember he took his time finishing that jazz, savouring each lungful. I remember the silence that fell and the stillness that settled through me. I remember the time was north... and

I remember his voice, close and warm and intimate.

'It's funny,' he said, 'but I'm not involved any more. I'm separate, and done. I've had my fill, and had enough. It's over now. It is the end… and time to die.'

We simply sat and stared, all the foulness of life seeping between us… And then it began.

He stood up wearily, turned and offered me his hand. I remember it was ever so slightly trembling.

'Come on,' he said, his voice wavering. 'Let's dance.'

I took his hand, and he held me in his arms, hugging me tightly in a warm embrace, and then we danced up the corridor and into the bedroom, whistling all the way – I recognized the tune immediately, it was 'Fly Me to the Moon'. Valerie and I danced to it on our wedding day. It was our first dance. A foxtrot. It was kind of him to remember. I carried on humming it as he found the Marks & Spencer bag and removed the two belts. My heart was racing… Suddenly everything seemed to be happening so quickly. There was activity and momentum. And it all seemed inevitable. He ran the brown belt through its buckle but didn't fasten it, just let it run along the length of itself past all the holes until it formed a natural noose. Then he ran the loose end of the brown belt through the buckle of the black belt and fastened it tight. Then he wrapped and firmly knotted the loose end of the black belt around the door handle on the outside of the bedroom door, and then threw the noose end over the top of the door, so that it hung down on the inside of the door. Then he put his hand through the noose and pulled hard – testing to see that it could take my weight. The noose tightened around my wrist and drew taut against the door as he pulled the weight of me up off the floor. The handle jerked and strained but held, and held fast.

'That'll do it,' he said, releasing the belt. 'Are you ready?'

I hesitated… Right now? I thought.

'Yes,' he said, stepping forward and slipping the noose around my neck… I stood perfectly still, and waited… Again I tried to remember – again I turned into the darkness and held her name and whispered, pleading, silently inward… Emma… Emma… But she didn't return. My legs fell out from under me, collapsing beneath the weight of me. I slumped abruptly forward and down. The belt snapped tight around my throat, viciously ripping into my neck, gagging me, cinched, throttled and choking – a terrible strangled scream lurched in my chest, Grade 7 trickled down my thighs and my penis stood swollen in testament. I was about to lose consciousness. I thought I had. He sank down harder onto my haunches, my eyes were rolling, a darkness gathered – a searing darkness of intense finality, engulfing everything… And then for a moment there was nothing, and then she was there, the top of her head beneath my nose – that smell that I'd forgotten – and her peeled clean skin, wriggling in my arms – her bright button eyes, shining – her petal pink cheeks, giggling – my fingers tickling, and kneading her, rolling her in my arms, squealing delighted shrieks of joy and a mad rash of kisses shared between… And then it stopped. And I was standing, coughing and spluttering, my head pounding, the noose loose, a burning welt throbbing around my throat, and tears in my eyes… I pulled the belts from around my neck and slumped onto the floor… He couldn't do it… the coward… He couldn't do it…

That was seven hours ago, and the craven little shuffler hasn't been seen since. He shat his pants and slinked away. I should have known, as a child he was always a bed-wetter... I've been waiting for him to return, but still he doesn't come... He has gone. And now I am alone, and it is late, both arms are up. My time is done. My week complete. And what a week it's been... glorious and awful, blessed and damned, never to be forgotten, or ever fondly recalled, but bright in the darkness. The seven days of Peter Crumb – first lost, and then found. But I digress, and tomorrow it may rain... The night is still full of life, and into it I must shuffle, and like the other slink away unseen. Yes ... I shall amble on, uncertain, not knowing where, but up and down, and to and fro... I'll find someone to follow and see where they lead. I'll skulk in the shadows and watch... I'll crumble on and wait... surviving and enduring... If they find me I will not be afraid. I'll dance and enjoy my moment in the limelight, and then he will return, and I will hear him drool that happy hello and sneer his tired good morning, and then I will remember, and I will return, and I will see her again... Yes, I will see her again...

I shall turn into a worm and disappear into the woodwork, silently chewing my way through the boards beneath your feet.

They're calling my platform – I must away. I'm moving on and chipping out. If you see me, don't say hello. Light a cigarette and smile, cross your legs and look away. Order some eggs and ignore me. I'm picking up the papers and beginning again. The headline this morning read:

# VIVA CRUMB